SPIES

SCOTT C. S. STONE

ST. MARTIN'S PRESS

NEW YORK

This is a work of fiction; any resemblance to persons living or dead is coincidental. The locales are real, and fondly remembered.

Copyright © 1980 by Scott C.S. Stone
All rights reserved. For information, write:
St. Martin's Press, Inc., 175 Fifth Avenue, New York, N.Y. 10010.
Manufactured in the United States of America.

Library of Congress Cataloging in Publication Data
Stone, Scott C. S.
  Spies.

  I. Title.
PZ4.S8793Sp   [PS3569.T642]   813'.54   79-27137
ISBN 0-312-75230-X

SPIES

for
Robert C. Miller,
Correspondent . . .
and one of the last free men

SPIES

PROLOGUE

He was wrinkled and bald, with white tendrils drifting from his chin, as if he had nestled his face in a cloudbank. He wore the thin cotton clothes of the village and had a dirty cloth tied around his head. His eyes were calm and strangely evocative of far places, of some Manchurian plain, perhaps, and his long, scraggly eyebrows almost masked the eyes that peered out at the world as if looking through the bars of a cell.

What he peered out upon was an Asian rain forest. He sat cross-legged on the rough wooden floor of the small shrine-sanctuary, listening to the driving rain on the thatched roof above him, and watched the pummeling the monsoon was giving the broad leaves and twisting vines of the thick and fecund jungle. He could see across the tops of many of the plants and bushes, although some trees soared above his hillside perch. In the distance he could glimpse the faint shimmering of the Mekong River, that brown artery that began in China and touched the land and the lives of much of Asia.

He sat there looking wise and slightly melancholy, wise in case the village children were sneaking up to watch him as they sometimes did; the melancholy was real. He had been constipated for days. Eating what the villagers brought him was part of the price of being the village holy man, the guru, and if occasionally it caused him discomfort, that was part of the guru business.

The leaden sky continued to hurl heavy pellets of rain against the jungle, and the rising and falling of the rain's intensity reminded him of the tide he had seen once on a beach far to the southwest, below Bangkok. He had been much younger then, embarked on a career as a pickpocket and hoping to marry. Her name was Pim. She worked at the White Christmas Massage Parlor in Bangkok. One day she disappeared with an American sailor off the USS *Manchester* and he never saw her again. Afterwards, he had given up his promising career and made his way to this poor upcountry village, where he was so overcome by sadness that he refused to eat, refused to work, and simply lay around on a mat with a bunch of mangy village dogs, scratching fleas and sighing with heartbreak. It was so compelling a performance that after three weeks the villagers decided he must be touched by a god, and so declared him a holy man. They had put him in charge of the newly constructed shrine-sanctuary which had been built on a hillside a mile or so above the village. There he had spent much of his life, cultivating the aura of omnipotence so necessary to a top-quality guru, and picking up the odd homilies that he launched at the villagers when they came for advice.

The villagers consulted him often, and treasured his wise and wonderful sayings. They liked his combination of worldliness and detachment; he could speak in several languages, learned in the Bangkok streets, but often he refused to say anything at all. He could be gentle but also stormy, and his moodiness was interpreted as a sign of high intelligence. The villagers also knew that occasionally he picked a pocket, just for practice, but the victim was never from their own village.

He was a venerable old man to the village children, who had learned to test his moods. If he were jovial the children would gather around him and ask for stories. He would tell them how the Supreme One created good people, who were simple villagers, and evil people, who were American sailors. Once in a while there would be an exotic visitor to the village and the children would lead the visitor to the guru. It might be the headman of another village seeking a cure for impotence ("It's all in the mind") or an officer from the small garrison in Khon Kaen looking for a village girl as a bride ("Find one who can cook.").

The guru seldom strayed from the shrine, confining his infrequent visits to nearby villages, or over to the Mekong to sit and watch the river traffic. Only once in his long stay at the shrine had he ventured on a trip of any significance, and that was back to Bangkok for a weekend.

He had gone out of curiosity, and had been appalled. There were fewer boats on the *klongs* but an astonishing increase in the number of cars and motorscooters on the streets. He had wrinkled his nose in disgust, but felt better a short time later after slipping the wallet from the pocket of an American sailor. He decided to spend the money before going home again, having already concluded that home truly was back in the north, away from the city he had used to love.

He went to a highly advertised and expensive restaurant, and got in after some argument about the way he was dressed. But he left a few minutes later when someone suggested he eat snails. He wandered around the corner and into a theater. When a duck in a sailor suit came on screen and started talking, he got up and walked out.

That night he fended off two hookers, a number of taxi drivers, and a shifty-eyed man with a box of stolen jewelry for sale. Renting a hotel room, he found the bed too soft to sleep on, and he resented the way the windows were made so they could not be opened. He couldn't feel the breeze or sniff the air. The following morning he handed the rest of the money to a startled child carrying an enormous shoe-shine box, and then he had turned north. With a great sense of relief he started walking home.

The more he walked the more he appreciated his shrine. The country was, as always, vibrant and interesting, but it was also full of foreigners, full of people hurrying. Other gurus he met on his trek northward confirmed for him how dismal things had become.

The guru was called the Old One by the villagers, who called him that even in the days when he had hair. While the hand was still quicker than the eye, the body had gone comfortably to pudginess. He compensated by keeping his hands deft and his mind fertile, striving for a placid lifestyle. "There is no such thing," he told the villagers more than once, "as too much moderation."

The Old One had spent his days contemplating his navel until he could no longer see it, and his nights snoring blissfully on the floor of the shrine. The shrine contained no idol, no manifestation of a god, but was simply a retreat where villagers could go and hear pearls of wisdom, or sit and meditate.

Today the Old One was alone; the rain had driven the villagers indoors, and the darkening skies cast a mood of languid melancholy over the forest. No one had been to visit him. The sawmill on the other side of the village was quiet, although the elephants were still at work on a distant hillside, pulling timber out of the forests with heavy chains while their owners hunched against the force of the rain. The occasional forest tiger was in his lair, and even the snakes, the cobras and the murderous kraits, were affected by the gloom, and stayed in their hidden places.

The Old One's guts rumbled with false promise, as they had for days. He sighed and wondered what his life would have been like had he stayed in the city, and unconsciously he moved his head in the direction of Bangkok. And got a start.

A man was running up the narrow trail.

The Old One squinted. It was a young man, carrying a bundle and gasping for breath. He headed unmistakably for the small shrine, running as if he were chased by ghosts.

The Old One shifted. This looked serious.

The runner neared, and the Old One put on his mask of studied indifference, but he continued to watch the approaching young man. The runner definitely was not from the village. He wore city clothing, long pants and a white shirt. He wore a gold watch. The young man reached the edge of the shrine and paused, breathing hard. The rain hammered at him but still he stood there, chest heaving. He clutched the bundle and stared at the Old One.

The Old One, in turn, looked calmly at the young man. He was trying to remember a Chinese saying he had heard from a brothel owner in Maha Sarakham. Remembering, he said, "Life is a tiger that every man rides, afraid to stay on, afraid to get off."

The young man was very still, a flicker of fear in his eyes. The Old One racked his brain for something more.

"Praise the Lord and pass the ammunition," he said.

With a slight shudder the young man wrapped his arms tighter about the bundle.

"Get in out of the rain," suggested the Old One. The young man eased in under the thatched roof and sat on the floor, with little rivulets of water running from him. Whatever he was carrying was wrapped in dirty rags, but he handled it with care. For long moments he sat, trembling, recovering from his pounding through the jungle.

"Why do you seek the Old One?"

The young man spoke for the first time. "I did not . . . I did not know you were here. I was simply running away."

"We know the sound of two feet running," said the Old One, pleased with himself, "What is the sound of one foot running?"

"I do not understand," said the young man.

"Naturally."

There was a sudden bang of thunder and the young man started. The rain, the gloom, and the Old One's stare were spooking him badly.

"Listen," he said to the Old One. "Is it always this scary up here?"

"There are spirits on the wind," said the Old One sagely,

and was gratified to see the fear return to the young man's eyes. "Lot of spirits. Demons, too."

The young man shuddered and suddenly gestured toward the bundle. "It is because of this."

"Perhaps," said the Old One, his curiosity mounting. "A stitch in time saves nine."

"What?"

"A *tical* saved is a *tical* earned."

"I did not earn this," said the young man. "I stole it. No, I did not exactly steal it. I took it from one who stole it."

"Does the elephant trod the earth or does the earth rise to meet the elephant?" The Old One was growing eloquent.

"Is the flea living off the dog or does the dog exist to support the flea?" countered the young man, getting into the spirit of the conversation.

"I'll ask the questions," snapped the Old One. "What's in the rags?"

"This," said the young man, and with a dramatic sweep of his hands, threw back the rags.

The Old One looked. And looked. It was a long time before he spoke. "Is it real?"

"Yes," said the young man. "And now you see why I must be rid of it."

"Of course," said the Old One.

"They will put me in prison for a long time if they find me with it," the young man said.

"Naturally."

"So," said the young man thoughtfully. "I must dispose of it. I will throw it in the river."

"Of course."

"Unless," said the young man, slowly, "you want to keep it yourself. It is something you understand, you see."

"Are you advising the Old One?"

"No . . . no. It was a passing thought. It is because you . . . well . . ."

"Silence," ordered the Old One. "I must think."

The young man looked as if he were about to lie down,

6

but before he could, the Old One spoke again. "I will keep it."

A smile curled on the young man's face. "Thank you, Old One. Now I can go in peace."

"And where will you go?"

But the young man was moving; he swung down the three steps of the shrine and stepped back into the rain. As the torrents hit him he turned once more and looked at the Old One inside the shrine. "Thank you," he said again.

"Never wake a sleeping tiger," said the Old One, gravely.

The young man turned and trotted back down the trail and swung to the left, away from the village. The Old One knew he was going to cross the Mekong. He would never see him again.

He turned back to the object on the floor of the shrine. It sat there, inanimate, but radiating power. It was the real thing, the genuine, the original. He stared at it a long time, while the downpour thickened and the brief twilight of Southeast Asia broke over the shrine and quickly gave way to darkness, which dropped like a velvet blanket over the wet and restless jungle.

WASHINGTON

In Henderson Farley's mind he was the quick brown fox; he was lean and rakehell. He saw himself tanned and fit and with a face that bore scars of old battles, devastating to women who were attracted to the subtle scent of mystery and the graceful six-foot frame. When he uncoiled in his mind he was the superb natural athlete, the deadly and highly skilled killing machine.

When he uncoiled in actuality, Farley was more the puffing up of a breakfast roll. He was short, balding, and tending to fat. He had never killed anyone or beaten a woman off with a stick, or anything else. His mind, while far from sluggish, often wandered into strange corridors full of doors which opened on stranger rooms. For all his mental adroitness he gave full rein to his illusions about himself.

He had picked his own code name. In the meager correspondence launched from his office, he was known after that silent slayer, the fer-de-lance. He thought it matched his style, his personality. The creature who knew Fer-de-lance's interoffice secrets was his parrot, Phineas, who shared some of his master's hauteur. Phineas also shared his master's other very human trait: he loved a good belt at odd hours during the day.

As a result of this, the natural habitat of Fer-de-lance was redolent with the aroma of good Montrachet or knife-edged bourbon, and frequently pierced by the cries of Phineas, begging or complaining. It was enough to drive his associates crazy, or so they said over the years. And there had been plenty of years for them to say it.

Fer-de-lance had not handpicked his staff, as was common in these assignments, but he had accepted them with a kind of stoic grace. He was happy to have gotten the appointment to lead them instead of following someone else. He did pick their code names, staying with the reptile *leitmotif*. Addison, the second in command, was tall, craggy, malicious and petty. Fer-de-lance had assigned him the code name Adder. Both Fer-de-lance and Adder enjoyed the joke they perpetrated on a third staff member, Ken Coleman, who had become King Cobra, symbol of power and strength. Coleman was gay.

It was King Cobra who stood now before Fer-de-lance, his eyebrows drawn together in a characteristic frown of complaint. Fer-de-lance eyed him with distaste.

"Not enough to keep you busy, eh?"

"It isn't that."

"It isn't that *what?*" snapped Fer-de-lance.

"It isn't that I don't have enough to do . . ."

"That's not what I mean, you simple shit." Fer-de-lance narrowed his eyes, the Clint Eastwood look. He tried to make his lips thinner, which made his dimples more pronounced.

King Cobra gave in. "It isn't that, *Sir.*"

"Then why are you complaining?"

"It's Addison, *Sir.*"

"Adder, you mean?"

"Adder, *Sir.*"

Fer-de-lance studied him, toying with the idea of putting him on permanent night duty, while another part of his darting mind was beginning to dwell on having a midmorning libation. Perhaps a vodka martini, stirred, not shaken. King

Cobra, meanwhile, let his eyes wander around the office; his periodic views of Farley's attempts at decorating always made him feel superior. In a sudden silence he thought he heard Farley talking again.

"Sir?"

"Pay attention, you camel's breath. What's the complaint this time?"

"It's Adder. *Sir.* He keeps putting me on as night duty officer. You know how boring that is. And it keeps screwing up my outside activities." King Cobra's voice was a high-frequency whine.

"Screwing," fired back Fer-de-lance with heavy sarcasm, "is hardly the word, is it? Adder knows what he's doing so buzz off and let's try to remember why we're here. This isn't all fun and games, you know."

King Cobra looked puzzled. It *was* fun and games, everyone knew that. Everyone within the organization, that is. He couldn't see why he had to have less fun than anyone else, but perhaps silly old Adder was angry with him about something. Well, he was getting nowhere with Farley.

Phineas broke the silence with an ear-splitting shriek. Farley glanced at his watch, pointedly, and King Cobra started backing out of the office. "Well if you'll excuse me . . ." he began.

"Damned right," Fer-de-lance snapped. "You get the hell out of here and back to work." Phineas shrieked again and jerked at the chain that held him captive to the T-shaped stand. King Cobra turned and fled.

Farley eased himself out of the chair and padded to the far corner of his spacious office. He thought of it as the war room. He pushed back the French doors and looked with satisfaction at the bar and wine-rack he had requisitioned and hidden on the forms as a water fountain. He paused for a moment to glance in the nearby mirror. It was a mirror he had bought at enormous expense from a passing carnival. In the mirror he was tall and thin, and when he turned his head he could admire the strong profile. Unfortunately the mirror elongated his balding head somewhat, but he had learned to live with that. He thought of it as the way El Greco would have painted him. He sighed and turned away from the mirror. When his image disappeared he became short and fat again, and the profile took on the appearance of a cushion. Never mind. The mirror always gave him a lift, now to be complemented with a horn of mead, or something suitable. After a happy dilemma he selected and poured a Zinfandel, padded back to his desk and settled in the well-contoured chair. He ignored Phineas's imploring screams, and while the parrot danced in frustration, Fer-de-lance took his first sip of the day, and as he had so many times before, thanked Bacchus for making him a spy.

In his office across the corridor, Adder heard Farley's door slam and a staccato tapping of heels as King Cobra swished away. Adder smiled frostily, knowing that the faggy bastard had gotten his comeuppance. Moments later Adder heard Phineas scream for a drink. Phineas was the only bird Adder had ever known which could whine at such volume. Farley would be opening a bottle, now . . . and now settling back behind his desk. He would be reaching into the bottom right-hand drawer of his desk and pulling out the James Bond novels. *Let him get into it, and then hit him with the news.*

He had much to talk about.

Sometime during the night, while Cobra was sleeping on duty, they had received a message. That in itself was unusual, but the content of the message was startling indeed. Naturally, King Cobra had long ago misplaced the decoder so Adder had received the message the following morning and finally worked it out. The message lay before him now, terse but volcanic, a white sheet of paper contrasting sharply with the dust of his in-basket. At first he thought it was another of Farley's jokes, but after his laborious decoding he knew that even Farley would not have been so severe.

Adder recognized the name at the top of the page and as he decoded the message, he felt his heartbeat accelerate, his breath quicken.

From *them!* In spite of himself, Adder felt a quick rush of excitement. And a few minutes later he permitted himself a slight wrinkling of the corners of his mouth, undetectable to anyone else but constituting a belly laugh in Adder's cold and labyrinthine mind.

The stealthy Fer-de-lance had been caught. The whole thing was blown. Adder actually chuckled.

Farley would have a heart attack.

Or drink himself into oblivion.

Because it was just about the worst thing that could happen to Farley. Perhaps to all of them.

And yet . . . and yet . . . Adder felt a slight stirring of the blood, a subtle sense of danger, as in the old days when he had been an operative. It had lasted only a year, but it had brought him the one memory he could unveil in his mind without being sardonic about it. For one glorious year he had been a real agent, young and tough, laughing in the wind that blew along the Bosphorus, and the girl beside him, her blonde hair glinting in the early morning sunlight . . .

Hold on, Adder told himself. There was no girl and no foreign setting. *Don't demean one year of fruitful labor.* He had been the best file clerk in the business for one glorious year and they had let him carry a gun, and the reports he stole were classified Damned Secret. So his life had not been all a waste.

And may not be again. He looked at the message on his desk and once again there was the almost imperceptible crinkle at the corners of his mouth.

At long last, they had received an assignment.

HONG KONG

MacTavish awoke, grateful that he hadn't died while he was out. It was his usual first feeling, followed closely by the usual second one—the sensation that sometime during the night he had eaten a giant bird, whole, and his mouth was full of feathers. He seemed to be in the middle of a wind tunnel, but the fog in his head wouldn't permit a quick determination. Every time he moved his head he put his life in peril, so for a time he lay still and listened.

Finally he isolated the wind-noise. It was a number of voices, all talking at once and very loud. Cautiously he squinted at the light fracturing against his face and falling through the slits of his eyes. He opened his eyes wider and with a great start saw an airplane diving straight at him. He closed his eyes and waited for death. After a time he opened them again and saw the ceiling fan more clearly. He even saw the flies on it, and with a flash of the old intuition he knew precisely where he was: on the floor of a Chinese restaurant.

Slowly he turned his head to one side, encouraged when it remained attached. Someone was playing the 1812 Overture in his skull, the cannons firing back to front. He looked out on a sea of dirty ankles, and voices continued to break over him like a *tsunami,* threatening to carry him off. He closed his eyes again, brought his head back around, and started to take inventory. Both hands twitched, so his arms were still appended. His hair hurt. He moved each leg with great care, but it took a lot out of him. At length he was able to run his hands over his genitals and was extremely pleased to find them still a part of him.

Somewhere, like a voice from a fogbank, someone was calling him. "Please," he whispered, his voice a rasp, "please, for God's sake, don't shout anymore. I'm right here."

"I know where you are, you dummy, how you think I calling you?"

"Please," begged MacTavish.

The voice paused, but the tumult in his head continued. It was like trying to ignore death. He forced one eye open again and looked into the friendly, misshapen face of the Chinese he called Fu Manchu Two.

"You wanna get off floor?" Fu inquired, with a voice like Zeus.

MacTavish considered. "Yes."

"Good," grunted Fu. "You bothering my customers. My *paying* customers."

MacTavish thought about this for a time. "How long have I been here?"

Fu reflected. "Since 1965."

"I mean on the floor, Fu."

"Since 1966."

"Don't be a wiseass."

"Get up, MacTavish, then we talk." MacTavish clawed at a table with one hand and Fu with the other, trying to get vertical. Fu, good-humored, helped him as he weaved to his feet and lurched for the bar he had fallen from a lifetime earlier.

"Scotch," he gasped.

"No," said Fu. "Tiger Beer."

"All right, all right." The beer appeared and MacTavish tilted it toward the ceiling. A long time later he put it down and the hammering in his head diminished to something akin to the incoming tide.

"Another, Fu."

"Sure, MacTavish."

As he was sipping the third Tiger Beer, MacTavish felt competent to talk. It came out as a croak. "What happened?"

Fu had the true Chinese sense of drama, and he drew himself up to give MacTavish a significant and intense stare. "She steal you wallet, you dummy."

"Who did?" asked MacTavish, genuinely puzzled.

"That *kwai-loh* you bring in here last night."

MacTavish reached for his wallet, but even before he felt the empty pocket he knew Fu was telling the truth.

"Tell me," he whispered, "and bring another beer."

"You come in here last night with girl from New Zealand. You keep calling her Kiwi Cutie—you real dummy, sometimes—and she get you stinko and you pass out. Big mess when you fall. I feel you head, nothing break that. You break chair. You owe me twenny-five dolla, Hong Kong." Fu put another beer in front of MacTavish.

"Where'd the girl go?"

"I dunno. I dunno she had you wallet until later."

"How'd you know later?" MacTavish smiled through the warfare in his head. *Caught the crafty bastard, finally.*

"I catch ricksha man feeling you pockets. Beat hell out of him. Search him, search you to see what he take. Nothing on him, nothing on you. Chase him off. Let you sleep."

"Sorry for what I was thinking," MacTavish mumbled.

"You all right," Fu said. "Think good for drunk."

MacTavish raised his head to glare at Fu. "Who says I'm drunk?"

"Me," said Fu. "You deaf, too?"

"God damn it, Fu."

"Okay, MacTavish."

He took another pull of the beer and tried to think of something besides the drumming in his head. He wasn't a drunk but he sure liked to drink. Years ago, when he had worked on a newspaper in the States, it had seemed romantic and dashing to be the young alcoholic reporter with the brilliant if uncertain future and the melancholy air. He thought it gave him charisma. When he found out that almost every newspaperman in the world felt the same way it was a bitter disappointment. He continued to work at his trade, drifting from job to job and eventually working in a succession of desk jobs, which he hated. He detested being inside all the time but it was the way with newspapers. If you were any good as a reporter they gave you bugger-all money and a promotion instead, which put you inside and away from the action, cooped up in some goddamned building with a marble facade and an inside like the detention home.

MacTavish became a correspondent because the States began to look alike, everywhere, and he wanted to see other parts of the world. For a while the old romanticism came back, with the added color and excitement of the Orient. After a time in Asia, MacTavish had experienced every emotion he could name, and once again became jaded. But he was a good drinker and it seemed to ease the pain and before he had much time to think about it, MacTavish was living off his savings, constantly looking for freelance assignments, sponging off Fu Manchu Two, and hoping to write a best-seller as a way out of his economic swamp.

He lived in a back room at the How Far Inn. That wasn't its real name, just as Fu Manchu Two wasn't Fu's real name. Fu's name was Fu Tsi-koh, and the How Far Inn was really the Hu Fah Inn. Fu and the How Far Inn were deeply symbolic of China as far as MacTavish was concerned. Fu befriended a lot of the crazies who drifted through, and he, MacTavish, treasured his long-standing friendship with the little restaurant owner. But right now Fu was ignoring him for the other customers. He knew why. Fu didn't approve of any girls except Chinese girls. The others were barbarians.

MacTavish finished the beer and pushed back from the bar; his head was clearing enough to settle into a steady, hammering throb, and his eyes were open enough to catch Fu's fingers flying over the abacus. He was adding up the beers and the chair. Friendship didn't go *that* far.

As Fu looked up MacTavish flashed the upturned palms and upraised eyebrows that signaled his inability to pay. Fu frowned, but waved him away, and MacTavish walked cautiously, holding his head very straight, out of the restaurant and into the steamy Hong Kong night.

He was in Wan Chai, the magnet for every sailor, gambler, drifter, panhandler, hooker, itinerant painter, con man, and bum who managed to get as far as Hong Kong. It was known by reputation to the genteel colony of the Peak, who imagined the district to be worse than it actually was. While the jet setters of the Peak whiled away their hours above the clangor of the city, Wan Chai was the spawning ground for murders, trysts, robberies, innovative sex, fantastic food, better than average gin-mill drinks, and enough shady deals to make happy the heart of a Chinese landlord. MacTavish loved it. It was as romantic as getting slapped in the face with a fish, but he loved it. Someday it would become respectable and he would hate it then, and move on.

He walked farther than he thought he could because some of the old charm of this strange, sweaty city reached out and clutched him by the throat. He loved the noise and the smells, and laundry hanging from every terrace, the cacophonic Chinese music, atonal and shrill. He loved the rich, fecund aroma of the waterfront, the smell of fish, the scent of an ocean rolling across the bay and smacking against the bulwarks. He was spellbound by the lights and lanterns. If you stood around long enough in Wan Chai you would see splendors and murders, births and deaths, avarice and grand gestures. And you would see the prettiest whores, taking a trick with their backs against the brick walls, earning more in a week than they could earn in months on a hardscrabble farm. MacTavish loved the Chinese whores, and respected them for their sensibility. Better to sell part of yourself than have your parents sell all of you to some farmer who treated you like a slave and beat you with regularity.

MacTavish plodded along, feeling the sweat begin. He rubbed the stubble on his cheeks and looked down to see how dirty he'd gotten. Pretty dirty, but what the hell. He had forgotten all about the New Zealand girl as he moved on, immersed in an eternity of Chinese, tacking and jibbing his way through the marvelous streets of Hong Kong. There was nowhere, absolutely nowhere, he would rather be.

LANGLEY

The Deputy Director, Covert and Clandestine Activities, Central Intelligence Agency, sat in his office in Langley, Virginia, staring out the picture window at the Potomac. He did not see it; his eyes had glazed over and angry thoughts were zinging through his mind like tracer bullets.

It had been a humiliating day. First he had forgotten his pass and the guards would not let him above the first-floor entryway until his boss had come down and signed him in, taking full responsibility. A few minutes later he had gone back and picked up the briefcase he had forgotten in the entrance and he *knew* he had heard the guards snicker behind his back.

Then finally, he had gotten to read the contents of the report on his desk, and was even more embarrassed. How would he ever explain this? What could he do about it?

After a time he got up and moved through his office door and down the hallway toward the men's room. Stopping in front of the door, he knocked three times, waited a moment and again rapped three times. The guard inside the room opened the door and he walked through it and over to a lavatory. He washed his face in cold water and dried it on a paper towel. He paused and looked into the mirror, wondering again if it were a one-way design and if someone on the other side were watching him. He didn't care. He looked at his reflection, noting the low forehead and bulbous nose, the fierce eyebrows and the lips with their built-in sneer. It was the face of a professional wrestler or a used-car salesman. He walked back to the door and started to knock again, caught himself, pushed the door open furiously and strode back to his office, flinging himself into the large swivel chair behind his desk.

He was a career CIA man and as such had taken the tough assignments. When he was assigned collateral duty as manager of the CIA softball team, he dedicated himself to it even though he hated sports. When the team went down to defeat in the playoffs against a women's team from the U.S. Government Printing Office, he was removed as manager but no one could fault him for his efforts. He did not complain when the Agency named him liaison to Australian Naval Intelligence. When he arrived in Sydney to discover there was no Australian Naval Intelligence, the home office would not believe him. It had taken a call from the Agency to a large Australian tour company in New York to convince the home office and allow him to return to Langley. At no time did he gripe about the hardships. Chosen to escort a high-ranking Italian Communist on a tour of the United States he had complied willingly, even though he hated tomato sauce and had heartburn for a week. Last year he had failed to get a one hundred percent contribution to the Director's favorite charity, but was given the job again this year. Yes, he had had some of the tough ones and some of the big ones.

But this . . .

The report lay in front of him, slightly wrinkled where he had gripped the pages in frustration and disbelief. Oh, it was true all right . . . it was too logical not to be. Methodically, he started to read it again.

CLASSIFICATION: Astonishingly Secret.
ACTION PARTY: Addressee.
COPIES TO: Duty Officer, Librarian.
ORIGINATOR: Director, Covert and Clandestine Activities.
ADDRESSEE: Deputy Director, Covert and Clandestine Activities.
MESSAGE:

John, you're not going to believe this one, but it's another biggie for you. I know you've been a little gun-shy since those damned women upset our softball team 57–2, but I want you to handle this personally. It actually has two parts. The first part deals with an incredible story we've picked up from agents in Asia and from our librarian, who was leafing through the files one day and found . . .

He read through the first few pages. It was a difficult and dangerous assignment, all right, but it could be handled by professionals. The second part of the message involved him personally, because he had been in charge of the move from downtown Washington out to the new quarters in Langley.

. . . so you see, John, we'll have to put someone on it. You handle it, eh?

Now, here's the delicate part.

Do you remember the discussion we had years ago in trying to find a moving company to get our files and stuff out to Langley? Well, I have it on tape, anyway, but I'm thinking of erasing a bit of it. You might recall that we had a limited budget for the move and you suggested that you locate a moving firm and I let you go ahead. John, you might have been more careful.

Your report on the move relates how you went out and hired the Gospodin Moving and Trucking Company, and how on the appointed day our offices were swarming with large, laconic characters in red jumpsuits, loading our files into trucks. They were marvelous workingmen and they had the trucks loaded rather quickly.

Because they were so good, so quick, didn't you wonder why it took so long for them to get the files to Langley? And wouldn't it have been circumspect if we had sent a few agents along in the trucks? Even the librarian, Miss Brumley, who rode out on her Vespa, might have gone along in a truck and it could have changed the course of things. At any rate, it took a *hell* of a long time for the trucks to finally show up, but once they did the workers moved those files in great style and speed. No wonder. The bastards had what they wanted.

You see, John, it now develops that along the way the workers stopped and photographed our files. Yes, John, it's true. The Gospodin Moving and Trucking Company was a KGB operation, and we now know they have photographed our files. Didn't you even wonder about the name, Gospodin? It's Russian, John. It's polite Russian for "Comrade." John, the God damned *Comrade* Moving and Trucking Company drove the Central Intelligence Agency files from Washington to our new headquarters in Langley. I wish now we had counted the drivers and workers; they might still have a man or two wandering around here. It wouldn't surprise me, at this stage.

Now, this gets a little complicated.

While they were photographing our files they came across one file folder which the KGB decided was so delicate they couldn't let us keep it.

Instead of photographing it, they took it. (By the way, remind me to talk to Roscoe, down in the basement. The KGB has a new camera setup using men with glass eyes. The phony eyes are really cameras, complete with eyelid shutters, all triggered via a cord which resembles a hearing aid. The cord runs down the shirt and into a pocket where it can be clicked. If the agent is seen taking pictures, it's nothing more than a dirty old man with a hearing aid winking at people. Maybe Roscoe can come up with something similar. Put the computer onto all available one-eyed agents.)

But back to the problem. The file they took from us revealed that we had organized a sub-unit and not made use of it. We know what the file contains because of the big office products deal we made with the Russians recently. They wanted to modernize their offices, including the KGB *dacha* on the outskirts of Moscow, so we sent them some equipment and technicians to show them how to run the machinery. Good old Yankee know-how! One of our technicians ran off a bunch of copies for them, and somehow this particular file was among them. He managed to smuggle copies back to us by bribing the Colonel in charge with a pair of blue jeans. So now we know about one of our own units. Isn't that the damndest round-about way of doing things you've ever heard? We might as well be the Post Office Department.

The bottom line, John, is that we have to do something with this sub-unit, and frankly I don't know what. The unit was organized originally as an experiment to see if essentially mediocre personnel could perform to capacity when exposed to specified training routines. Unfortunately the psychiatrist in charge of the experiment left the Agency without leaving a forwarding address, and the unit sort of languished.

Oh, yes. The reason the file was taken is that it reveals the existence, in the unit, of a double agent. I'm surprised that the KGB left him in place so long. You don't suppose they forgot about him, too, do you? The silly bastards.

John, the problem in Asia demands immediate attention. The problem with the sub-unit is your baby too, but not as urgent. Remember, I have to take this to The Highest Levels and when I do I need to be able to say that we're taking appropriate action. Okay?

This report sent on recycled paper. Printed by U.S. Government Printing Office, all-Washington softball champions.

WASHINGTON

"An assignment?"

It was the fourth time Fer-de-lance had whispered those words, and Adder was enjoying every moment of it. He, Addison, had gotten used to the idea and now was amused at his boss's shock.

"From *them?*"

Adder nodded.

Fer-de-lance sat stiffly, or at least upright, in his chair. He was stunned. This was *real.* He threw a quick glance at the bar and thought better of it; no time to give Adder the wrong idea.

Addison caught the glance, but his face was immobile.

Phineas shrieked and both men jumped.

"Well, sir," Adder prompted, "we really should make some move or other, wouldn't you say?"

Farley was well back in his chair, which meant both feet were off the floor. He looked at his spit-shine as if there was an answer there somewhere. Finally, reluctantly, he said, "all right, what do they want?" When he said *they* he felt like standing at attention.

Adder licked his thin lips and for a moment really looked

like a snake. He read the entire message aloud to a frozen Fer-de-lance:

CLASSIFICATION: Unbelievably Secret.
ACTION PARTY: Addressee.
COPIES TO: Duty Officer, Originator.
ORIGINATOR: Deputy Director, Covert and Clandestine Activities, Central Intelligence Agency.
ADDRESSEE: Supplemental Unit, Infiltration & Tactics (SUIT)
MESSAGE:

Have discovered your existence. Forward at once complete report of all Intelligence/Infiltration/Tactical missions in preceding eighteen years. Also forward breakdown of present personnel reference duties, experience and pay scale. Upon forwarding this information, stand by for activation of unit and top priority assignment in Asian theatre where current professional operatives have been blown. Anticipate sending Asian expert to SE Asia for further orders. Prepare travel chits, penicillin, usual weaponry, cover, change of papers, etc. Assignment may be considered dangerous. What the hell have you been doing for eighteen years?

Burn after reading.

Farley looked up, startled. "Burn?"

"He means the message . . . sir," Adder said.

"Of course, of course. A little Intelligence humor, there, Adder. But I forgot, you don't have a sense of humor, do you?"

Addison mulled it over.

"Never mind, never mind. The questions are, why did they suddenly remember us, and who are we sending to Asia?"

Adder sighed. "Some snoopy file clerk got onto us, I suppose. What will you tell them we've been doing for eighteen years?"

Farley thought. "Training."

"I see," said Addison, and almost smiled.

Farley said the hell with it and bounced out of his chair and hurried to the wine cellar. *Let Adder think what he wanted to think.*

"Join me in a drink?" To his surprise, Adder said yes. A few moments later the two men were sipping the Zinfandel. Phineas went into a paroxysm of piercing screams, but was ignored.

It was Addison who, shouting above the parrot, hung the second question out for consideration: "Who are you sending to Asia?"

"Arlington Veto . . . Viper."

"Out of curiosity, why?"

"He speaks the language, hey?"

"He speaks Japanese. This assignment is Southeast Asia."

"So?"

"They aren't the same."

"I know that," Fer-de-lance said patiently.

"Then I don't understand."

"If you can speak one of those crazy languages, you can learn the other in a few days, Adder. Don't you know anything about Intelligence?"

Adder merely glared.

"All right, who would you send?"

"You."

Fer-de-lance started to protest, then stopped. Why not? It couldn't be *that* dangerous. It might be more dangerous to try to tell the CIA why a unit like this one had been inactive for eighteen years. The DDCC would never believe the truth: they had been formed, their files tucked away somewhere, and promptly forgotten about. Their pay checks and automatic raises had come through, regular as clockwork. That they had made no protest probably would be held against them, though. Farley sniffed. It wasn't *his* fault he hadn't received any assignments before. He was ready, wasn't he? Let Adder explain all that to the CIA. He, the deadly and fearsome Fer-de-lance, would pull off this Asian caper and return with the booty, whatever it was, and let the devil take the hindmost.

"What?" asked Addison.

"What?" echoed Farley.

"You were muttering."

"You know, Adder, I think you're right."

"Of course I'm right. I heard you distinctly."

"No, no, no. I mean about me going to Asia."

"Wonderful," prompted Adder. "Want me to arrange things?"

"Yeah . . . and, uh, Adder. Prepare a report on our training for the CIA. Make it . . . you know . . . good."

Adder gave a slight nod, and quickly left the room.

"Well, Phineas," said Fer-de-lance. "It's derring-do in the Orient." He walked to the mirror and stood before it for long moments, practicing his sinister look.

HONG KONG

The antipode of Wan Chai, where Mac-
Tavish was stumbling happily through the quickening dusk,
was the Journalists' Club, high in a starched and pressed
hotel. It was all the things Wan Chai and MacTavish were
not—clean, proper, respectable, and predictable. The Club
gleamed with the sincerity of real silver, and the soft lighting
and tasteful carpeting, the hum of Important Conversation,
all combined to make the visiting correspondent feel he had
somehow wandered into the private preserves of an Arab oil
prince. Chinese waiters in stiff whites stood poised to answer
every whim of the fortunate patrons. The indoor plants were
healthy, a sure sign of wealth. On the far wall of the Club the
broad mahogany bar was topped by rows of crystal and the
bartender knew which wine went into which glass. More and
more the Club was frequented by men in jackets and ties,
and the old Hong Kong uniform of bush jacket and scuffed
shoes was a rarity in the Club, and frowned upon by the
regulars.

MacTavish had visited the Club once, more or less falling
out of the elevator which had rocketed him twelve stories
and then flung open its doors to reveal him to the Club and

the Club to him. Both were appalled. He stood there, disheveled and slightly drunk, peering into the soft lighting, while the denizens of the Club stared back stiffly, thanking God they worked for wealthy newspaper chains or television networks. MacTavish heard the collective intake of breath, knew they were afraid he was actually going to enter the immaculate interior and stand at the bar. He felt as strange as if he had landed on the surface of the moon. He sensed the waiters moving uneasily in his direction and felt the coldness of the stares. At the same time he was disgusted by the antiseptic faces and the sterility of the Club, and found it hard to believe these were his colleagues. Standing there he heard the elevator open behind him and he quickly backed into it, still staring at the opulence before him. He had the urge to take off his pants, or yell obscenities, and as if in anticipation the elevator doors flicked to a close and the elevator plummeted back to the street. From the sidewalk he stood looking up at the twelfth floor. He felt like Tensing Norkey might have felt, coming off Everest and gazing back at it. Later, when he thought about the Club it was with wonder. Were there real people in there? What did they talk about? Did they ever get drunk, get laid, get shot at? Did they ever get dirty, have malaria? MacTavish could see them in the Asian bush, never sweating, never swatting at mosquitoes. They probably traveled in transparent, air-conditioned bubbles.

And what the hell did they *write* about?

MacTavish had shaken his head and moved off obliquely to the waterfront, the dirty, charming, raucous waterfront which was, above all else, alive.

In the Club they had dismissed MacTavish's brief visit as a ripple on the calm surface of their lives, much the same way they ignored the typhoons which periodically smashed the island, and the same way in which they ignored the pirates who now and then turned up in brief, explosive encounters with merchant junks up from Singapore. They were concerned with loftier matters, affairs of state. They seldom bothered with anyone of lesser rank than a Minister, and their interviews were conducted in gentlemanly fashion. Many of their "think pieces" began with "The Prime Minister told me today . . ." or "In an exclusive luncheon at his home yesterday, the Minister of the Interior . . ." The intimate soiree was a mother lode of news, and it was not unheard of for the correspondents to interview each other. Naturally, a lot of them were television reporters and most of the others worked for fat newspaper chains or syndicates. They were well known, to the point that other newsmen met them at airports and requested interviews. At least one or two of them traveled with secretaries.

Among the correspondents there were enough jealousies and petty hatreds to satisfy a reunion of the Borgias, but much of the pure envy was directed at one man who sat at his special table in the northwest corner of the Club. He wore clothes tailored in London, shoes from Switzerland, a large sapphire from Thailand. He wore a practiced charm which had seen him through tense situations and two decades of image-building.

Sidney Stratton was one of the most famous television reporters in the world. The handsome head, with its jet-black hair and distinctive gray temples, its warm brown eyes, and calm and knowing look, had been seen at one time or another by millions of viewers around the world. Everyone knew he was a step away from becoming a great television essayist. A very few people knew that Stratton hardly ever covered a hard news story himself—that was a dirty, smelly business left to the archaic print journalists and the new kids at the network who had to win their spurs on the battlefields.

Stratton's usual point of view was the Olympian one of logic and calm reason. He radiated the idea that if the world would simply listen to him for a while he could straighten it all out. He would, too, someday. But right now he was in the thick of it (he suggested to his viewers), telling the world what was happening in its capitals. To listen to Stratton was to believe that only he had the right answers; to view him was to reinforce that belief and wonder why this man wasn't Emperor. Sleek and coiffed, Stratton lounged elegantly in the Club and worked appreciatively on a rum and Coke amid the stares of lesser newsmen, some of whom wondered aloud how much the network was paying him. (It was more in a year than some of them would earn in five or six. It was six times the salary his cameraman was paid, the equivalent of all the Club's waiters' annual salaries, the price of three yachts in any shipyard out in Aberdeen, three times the salary of the ranking member of the American consulate, including his cost-of-living 'allowance, eleven times the salary of many shirtsleeved editors in the American Midwest, and more than all but one or two American poets ever earned from their art.) Stratton was one of the few newsmen anywhere who owned a Rolls-Royce, first-named the President of the United States, and had never read a word of Walter Lippmann.

He knew he was envied; he regarded it as a compliment.

Calling for his second rum and Coke, Sidney Stratton mused about his next reporting piece. Years ago the network had given up making assignments for him. Now he flitted about doing the things that interested him—almost always high-level political or economic stories. His last few had been so esoteric that he felt it was time to get in closer touch, figuratively speaking, with the great unwashed public, so he'd better do something for the little people. He examined and rejected several possibilities. To do a story on the Hong Kong water people would mean getting out on a foul fishing boat. He dismissed that quickly. To handle properly the recent rioting out in North Point could be a bit dangerous, and who needed that? Of course he could bash over to Bangkok and call on his old friend, the Minister of Tourism . . . were there any festivals in Bangkok this time of year? Or he might drop in on Lee Kwan Yew's Singapore, a much nicer place now that they had cleaned up the streets. He *might* do a follow-up on the geisha training program he had so beautifully reported on in Kyoto, but then it was a tiresome time to be flying. Something closer to home. Well, it would come to him soon. He ordered a third rum and Coke.

Studying the menu with mild disappointment, Stratton was aware of the oncoming glide of the maitre d', who was a tyrant to the staff and servile to the correspondents. Stratton approved of him enormously. "A telephone call for you, sir," the man whispered deferentially, in the soft sibilants of South China.

"I am dining," Stratton said formally.

"Ah . . . yes, sir. I believe it is New York for you, sir."

"Perhaps you didn't hear me. Tell them to call back after dinner."

"Ah . . ."

Stratton affected his patient and knowing air. "Is this insubordination, Wong? Must I speak with management about your services?"

Wong began shuffling backward. "They said it was an emergency, sir. An assignment. Most sorry, sir."

"Disappear," Stratton ordered curtly, and Wong fled.

Turning back to the menu, Stratton bowed his great intellectual gifts to the problem at hand. Begin with the caviar or the smoked salmon? An assignment? Move quickly over the soups, which actually featured a damnable Chinese egg-drop soup. Wogs. A *salade,* of course. Who could be calling him from New York? Kingsley, the network president? Probably the dressing actually wasn't Roquefort. Perhaps they were relaying a message from the Secretary of Defense. Better stay with the oil and vinegar. His last piece had dealt with Japan's marvelous railway system, so maybe the Secretary of Transportation had a question or two. The Stroganoff was tempting, but then so was the filet mignon.

He looked up, suddenly irritable. The telephone call had upset him. He snapped his fingers for a fourth rum and Coke and contemplated calling the New York office. No, better not. Better not set a precedent. He turned back to the menu.

Is it possible that the President . . . ?

Stratton looked at his eighteen-hundred-dollar Rolex, trying to remember if New York were ahead or behind, and gave it up. Irritably, he smashed the napkin down on the linen tablecloth and stood up. So he would call them, for once. It never hurt a great man to show a little humility from time to time. He'd make damned sure they noticed it.

THE JUNGLE

The Old One felt better. He was, in fact, almost cheerful. The constipation had cleared up miraculously, once he had gotten rid of the object the young man had dropped on him.

At first he had left it in the shrine, sitting carelessly in the corner with the rags covering it. Then the villagers had gotten too curious; after all, a holy man does not covet material possessions. He had let them wonder about it for a while, then he started thinking about what to do with it. It was a challenge, all right, especially for one who had seldom stirred more than a mile or two from the shrine for so many years.

In the end it was simple, as all great ideas are. And in time the object was safely out of sight, and out of mind. In a while the Old One did not think of it more than a few times a day, and he was happy to be returning to his routine. The village children brought him a large, dead, blackbird and he made up horrifying stories about spirits who inhabited the bodies of birds and carried off wayward children. The village tax collector paid him a courtesy call and went away empty-handed, as usual, but not before the Old One had lifted a few *baht* from the man's shirt pocket. Once, in the late afternoon, a fisherman from the far-off seacoast stopped by, a man the Old One had known many years before. From the fisherman the Old One heard many new expressions he would remember carefully and use as the occasion arose. The fisherman, uncomfortable with this strange old man so unlike the young pickpocket he had known, left without spending the night.

But mostly the old man sat and stared out at the jungle, the wild, fetid, complex, and unstructured world that spread before him. He listened to the piercing cry of the strange and exotic birds and often he heard cries of pain, whispers of warning. Once or twice he had heard the grunt of a great beast as it launched itself at its prey, and the swift, sharp flurry as the prey died in the desperate struggle. Now and then the Old One would hear lovers in the bush, and smile to himself and remember Pim, her knowing hands and the deep, wild look she flashed in lovemaking.

After a time he didn't think about the stolen object at all.

HONG KONG

Natalya got out of the cab and entered the bakery, followed by appreciative stares. As she passed through the bakery and up the steps to the second floor, there were more stares. She had grown accustomed to them; for the last ten years of her life, she had realized she was a truly beautiful and unaffected woman. She enjoyed the hell out of it.

And she was enjoying today. The prospects of a new assignment were enough to set the blood tingling and bring color to her cheeks. An assignment meant fun, lots of money to spend, a certain amount of deliberate deception, and—rarely—a *little* danger. She didn't mind a *little* danger. The worst part of it all was her control, who waited for her now on the second floor of the bakery.

She reached the top of the stairs and glanced around the room. It was a Russian restaurant, the best in Hong Kong, but it was damned near a secret, for there were no signs, no directions, and no advertising. It was reached through the bakery below, which had no connection with the restaurant itself, as far as she knew. It was the traditional meeting place with Boris, and while she loved the restaurant, she hated Boris.

She caught his eye. He was sitting at a corner table. *Melodramatic to the end,* she thought. She moved catlike across the floor to his table and was amused to see his cold facade start to crumble. Boris was in love with her, or lusted after her, and she alternately gave him line and reeled him in, for her own amusement.

"Well, Natalya, as lovely as ever."

"Well, Boris." She sat and looked at him. It had been weeks since she had seen him last.

Boris was bald and bearded. He looked like the typical circus strongman, and his leer was as malevolent as the smile of a shark. He was enormous, and even sitting down he gave the impression of speed and power. As she studied him she suddenly realized there was something more than usual ricocheting around in his head.

"An aperitif?"

"A drink," she agreed. Boris signaled and a waiter appeared. She ordered vodka and sat back in the high-backed rattan chair, waiting for Boris to launch her on a new adventure. As she watched he seemed to rumble; then he exploded in a laugh that carried across the room and out into the street.

"What *is* it, Boris?" But he was lost in it now, the tears rolling down his cheeks and his huge frame shaking with mirth.

"Ah-ha," he wheezed, "Ah-ha, ah-ha." And he exploded again.

"For God's sake, Boris."

He wiped his eyes. "Forgive me. There often isn't much to laugh about in this business of ours. Ah-ha. You see, Natalya, we have a new assignment, that is, we are to *counter* an assignment the Americans have received. Ah. That's better." He sipped his own vodka as her drink arrived, and settled back in his chair.

"You see," he began, "the mischief-making American Intelligence forces are beginning, once again, their meddling in the internal affairs . . ."

"Boris, *please.*"

"Oh, well. Would you like to order, then?"

"Yes. The veal. And more vodka. Then tell me without all the propaganda."

Finally, he did. "Eighteen years ago . . . ah-ha, ah-ha . . . eighteen years ago the Americans formed a sub-unit of their Intelligence forces. They called it Supplemental Unit, Intelligence and Tactics. A month after they formed it on paper, they collected a staff, rented a building, set up the procedures and code-processing departments, and . . . ah-ha . . . they forgot about it."

She looked up, startled. "Forgot about it?"

"Yes. It has been unused for eighteen years."

"But what have they been doing?" Boris exploded again, and Natalya found herself caught up in it. She began to shake with a wonderful, hearty laughter.

"They have . . . they have . . ."

"Yes . . . yes . . . ?"

"Ah-ha . . . they have been . . . *in training!*"

It was a long while before the two of them grew calm enough to talk.

"Well," Natalya said. "And they were getting paid, and everything?"

"Yes. They collected regular pay, and regular pay increases. They neglected to notify their parent unit that they were still in business, and life simply went on around them. The staff is a joke and the agent in charge must be seen to be believed."

"What has this to do with us?"

"Well, my dear Natalya. At last the unit has been discovered, and immediately given an assignment. We have been given the assignment of foiling their assignment."

"I don't understand."

"All in good time. For now, we must prepare you for your duties."

"Prepare?" she asked, warily.

"Yes. As you are a natural *femme fatale,* as the French say, I want you to get to know a certain American here in Hong Kong. It will be very easy for you to get next to him, as the Americans say, but if he finds out what you're up to, it won't be all beer and skittles, as the . . ."

"I know, I know, the English. But what am I supposed to do, and who is the American?"

"Listen closely," said Boris, and he leaned over her conspiratorily. "This man will be a challenge."

As he talked, she nodded. It *would* be a challenge. "How do we find him?"

"He is a correspondent, after all," Boris intoned. "Besides, I have done my job. We reach him through Chow Fun."

"Chow Fun is a noodle," said Natalya. Boris smiled.

A day later Chow Fun—the man, not the noodle—was looking for MacTavish. He knew finding him wouldn't be easy.

Chow Fun was the essence of China: tough, taciturn, wily, and shrewd. He also was given to moments of wild cackling, being possessed of and by a truly whacko sense of humor. It was one of the reasons he loved MacTavish. MacTavish made him laugh.

He loved MacTavish for a lot of other reasons, dating back to the time MacTavish had come to his aid in a bar brawl. Later, Chow Fun had brought MacTavish a girl to sleep with, by way of thanks, and MacTavish had obliged without finding it strange or "Chinese." MacTavish had lent him money, borrowed it back, gambled it away, and never kept score. MacTavish was dissolute and becoming degenerate in one view, or becoming very much his own man in another view. The latter view was Chow Fun's own explanation for MacTavish's drinking bouts, his whoring, and his gambling.

The gambling probably was in MacTavish's past—he had very little money these days, and if it became a choice between gambling and drinking, MacTavish would drink.

Chow Fun knew where to look for MacTavish. If MacTavish had a lot of money, he would have to go to Macau to look for him. If MacTavish were totally broke, he would be in his room at the How Far Inn, smashing at a battered typewriter in an effort to produce something someone would buy.

If MacTavish had *some* money, the situation became more complicated, and Chow Fun bent his mind to the problem.

Supposing, he mused, that MacTavish were drunk. He would be either a happy drunk or a sad drunk. If he were happy, he would still be drinking in one of the thousands of Wan Chaibars, and Chow Fun had an all-week task in front of him. If he were sad, he could be in many places. He could be sitting on the curb across the street from where the old Gloucester Lounge used to be. It had been MacTavish's favorite place in all of Asia before it was torn down to make room for a high-rise. MacTavish's other favorite place was gone too, so he might be there, up on the Peak, sitting on a rock and contemplating the place where the old Correspondents' Club had afforded booze, companionship, news, and gossip. MacTavish might be over on Lan Tau Island, in one of the fisherman's cottages, sleeping off a long binge. Or he might be in the little restaurant up near Castle Peak, eating prawns with a sprinkling of ginseng to keep up his virility, in a sexy-sad mood in which all women were his sweethearts and all deserved his love.

Another, but remote, possibility was that MacTavish would be working on a story somewhere. Chow Fun, through his knowledge of MacTavish and his ways, had become familiar with the exigencies of reporting. He knew that MacTavish could have been sent off on a moment's notice to cover a story somewhere, a war in some other part of Asia, or the battles over the opium crop in South Asia. It was possible, but not likely. MacTavish didn't get many assignments like that anymore. The thought of it made Chow Fun laugh, but it was rueful laughter. Poor MacTavish.

Poor MacTavish. He was a man with great talents, and yet he was never quite happy. Chow Fun did not believe all whites were barbarians, but he thought them all destined for unhappiness. They were strange people. They burned their food before eating it. They professed to like their drinks, but they poured strange things in with them. Their women were milk-white and loud, which may have been why most of the men were deferential. But not MacTavish. He was sensible, and preferred Asian whores because there were no entanglements later on. MacTavish, Chow Fun suspected, wasn't all white. So, maybe, MacTavish was still somewhere in Wan Chai.

He padded down the street, looking in at the various bars. He thought there must be an aircraft carrier in the bay, because the bars were overrun with American sailors, all incredibly young and healthy. He lost count, after a while, and began to reassess. If MacTavish were reasonably sober and reasonably affluent, he might have picked up a girl of reasonably pliant morals and taken her off to dinner in one of the floating restaurants at Aberdeen, on the other side of the island.

Discouraged, Chow Fun moved on through the evening, surrounded by the familiar sights and smells of the waterfront. As he left yet another bar, he stood on the street outside, trying to get his eyes adjusted for the hundredth time to the sudden darkness after the light of the bar. He was blinking when a hand shot out and grabbed him by the neck and held him immobile. He felt a pressure in the small of his back, and stood very still.

"Stand still. Dis is Louie, and if ya make a move I'll blow you fulla beer with dis twelve-ounce San Miguel."

Chow Fun turned and looked down at the beer bottle and up at MacTavish's pleasantly twisted face. Chow Fun broke into laughter. "MacTavish."

"Yeah."

"Where you was?"

"You mean, where I were? Ain'tcha ever gonna learn the language, you heathen Chinee?"

"Listen, MacTavish. A *job* for you."

MacTavish reeled over the little Chinese. "Listen, Chow Fun. *You* listen. On a Richter scale of drunk I am eight point five, and I am in no condition and no mood to work. Comprendez-vous?"

"Much money, MacTavish."

"How much?"

"Much."

"Yeah?"

"MacTavish, this *kwai-loh*, a woman. She come to see me, looking for you. Fu send her. He look for you, too. She has much money and she want you to work for her."

"No."

"Eh?"

"I don't work for women."

"This one, MacTavish. She prettiest woman in Hong Kong. I swear. I swear by Jesus Christ, by Joe Namath, by Ernest Hemingway."

MacTavish's brow wrinkled. "This is serious, huh?"

"Much, MacTavish."

"Well, let's go, man."

"First you clean up?"

MacTavish looked down. His pants were wrinkled and soiled, and his bush shirt looked as if a tank had rolled across it. He felt the stubble on his face and could taste the booze fumes in his mouth. "I feel like the Russian Army camped in my mouth last night," he said.

"That's she. Russian."

"What?"

"Russian lady. A beauty, I swear."

"Are you kidding me?"

"By Jesus Christ, by Joe Namath, by . . ."

"Okay, okay."

Something massive, something latent, moved in the back of MacTavish's mind. This could be serious. Tass? *Pravda?* Would he write for them? Is that what's up? He looked down at Chow Fun's open, inquisitive face. "I would," said Mac-Tavish, slowly, "write for Jack the Ripper if he had the money."

"Clean up, yeah? Then we go."

"Screw it. They take me the way I am, or not at all. A man has to have some pride, you know?"

"Then you come now."

"Let's go."

MacTavish explored his pockets: a bill from the Hotel of the Wondrous Apollo on Lockhart Road; a penknife of uncertain origin; a set of keys so old he couldn't remember what they were for; a stub from the Happy Valley racetrack; a note from No-Squeak Chun that his shoes were ready; and about eight or nine dollars, Hong Kong.

"How far is it?"

"I have money," Chow Fun explained.

"Good," grunted MacTavish. "A taxi, my man."

The taxi took them through town and up toward the Peak. It was October, and the best time of year in Hong Kong. MacTavish sat back and enjoyed the ride. In the pleasantly swaying car he put his head back and looked out through narrowed eyes on his adopted home. The confusion and color of Wan Chai had faded to the more respectable and businesslike interior, and now the car was taking them past a lot of shrubbery and soft exterior lighting. As they wound nearer the top MacTavish sat up; this *was* serious. They were getting into the big-money preserves.

They got out of the cab in front of a house that might have been lifted from the English countryside. It was huge, clean, and expensive. It was surrounded by a very formal garden and more trees than anywhere else on the island.

Chow Fun hung back to stay with the car and driver. Mac-Tavish ambled forward through a massive moon gate and found himself facing a wrought-iron barrier with a telephone to one side. He picked up the telephone and waited. A crisp, Chinese voice, female, asked his name in impeccable English.

"MacTavish."

"Your full name?"

"MacTavish."

He put the telephone back and waited. The gates slid open and he strolled forward, up the steps and to the door. He was reaching for it when it was opened by a young Chinese girl, and her eyes widened slightly at the sight of him.

"Please come in. My mistress will be with you in a moment." But it was even faster. Natalya was moving down a curving stairway, and she sent her voice in a friendly greeting.

He looked up and froze. She was medium-sized and curved. She was tawny and feminine. She wore something blue in Thai silk that was the perfect shade for her smooth, brown skin. He got a flash of Mongolia in the slightly tilted eyes, and a flash of humor in the uplifting corners of her splendid mouth. Her voice had come to him in a lilt, with an accent that he found charming. When she got closer to him, he looked into eyes that reminded him of perfectly cut emeralds. As he continued to look, Natalya smiled, and he was lost.

"Come and sit, and have a drink with me. My name is Natalya Vorshova, and I want to talk with you about a job."

Anywhere you fancy, MacTavish thought.

She led him into a large, well-furnished room. He wondered again where she got her money, for she was in one of the finest homes in Hong Kong. They sat on a large, curving sofa and a young Chinese man in evening clothes appeared at once. "Tao, vodka for me, please, and whatever Mr. MacTavish would like."

MacTavish cleared his throat and spoke for the first time. "Scotch," he said. He turned back to Natalya. "Well, Miss Vorshova, you sure passed one test. You didn't ask me how come I look so scroungy at the moment."

"Just Natalya. And it's none of my business, Mr. Mac-Tavish."

"It's your business if you're thinking of hiring me."

"And do you have other tests?"

He bit his tongue, and tried not to think about it. Tao reappeared and MacTavish swallowed the first soothing taste of the scotch. However this turned out, he was enjoying the beginning. Natalya was sitting so he could get a better than average view up the blue dress to smooth, bare thighs. The lighting was subdued but not immoral, and the drink was helping to clear his head. For a split second he wished he *had* cleaned up before coming here.

She smiled as if reading his thoughts. *I'm glad she can't read them all.* "Listen," he said. "About this job."

Natalya smiled and lifted her chin. "Can't we talk about it later? After dinner?"

"Well . . ."

"Did you have other plans tonight?"

"No, but . . ."

"Would you like to clean up here, Mr. MacTavish?"

There was what MacTavish would describe as a pregnant pause, and she continued: "I'm sure we can find a robe or something for you. You can use the guest room at the top of the stairs. Tao will show you the way. Please order another drink if you like, and join me here when you've finished. Perhaps you will be hungry by then."

He stood, and watched as the Russian girl uncoiled with pure grace and moved to stand in front of him, still holding her drink. "There's a shower in your room, but if you prefer, there's a rather unusual bath at the end of the hall. Tao can show you, if you like."

MacTavish had the uncomfortable feeling he was being led, and perhaps enjoying it too much. "I'll take the shower," he mumbled, peering down at her. *God, what a beauty.* "The bath another time, okay?"

"Certainly, Mr. MacTavish." She smiled. He felt like Adam watching his first sunrise.

Tao materialized at his side. MacTavish ordered another Scotch. As Natalya turned to leave he headed for the stairs and the room at the top. Climbing the stairs he began to have doubts. He had known some weirdo stories and most of them started off a lot seamier than this one. Anything that started on this level was bound to drop, somewhere. How did she get onto him anyway? —a question he had meant to ask her from the start. Damn, she was distracting, though. Uh.

The room was as impressive as the rest of the house. The high ceilings and extravagant space spoke of big money and MacTavish began to feel better. The shower was as luxurious as everything else he had seen and he gloried in it. A few minutes later he found a razor and an old-fashioned shaving mug and brush. And in the closet he found a kind of light-weight caftan made of some kind of gauze from India. He threw his dirty clothes on the bed and climbed into the pale blue caftan, the first he had ever worn. He looked at himself in the mirror, noting the new wrinkles around his eyes and the gray beginning above his ears. He had the sudden feeling he would die in Asia. He sure as hell meant to *live* till then, though, and smiling, he pushed through the door and down the stairs. He was glad Chow Fun couldn't see him in a dress.

"You look very nice, Mr. MacTavish," Natalya said. "Would you like another drink or are you hungry?"

"Hungry as a damned bear," he said, grinning. She led him into a dining room that would have housed a dozen Chinese families, and gestured toward a table the size of a small yacht. There were two places set, but not at the ends. They were close together, and she waved him to a seat at the head of the table and sat close by on his right. Tao began to serve.

MacTavish had a fleeting impression of elegance, then tried not to think about it too much. It was overwhelming, but even then it couldn't compare with the shining eyes of this mysterious Russian girl. The candlelight gleamed in her hair and her smooth, flawless skin, and he stared una-shamedly at the curve of her lips as she smiled gently at him.

"Potage Crème de Champignons," she said, the accent perfect. Tao was placing the soup in front of them. "Will you pick the wine?" At exactly that moment one of the largest and fiercest-looking men MacTavish had ever met came through the door. "This is Boris," she said. "He looks after the wine cellar, and other things."

MacTavish looked up . . . and up . . . into the expressionless eyes. He formed an instant dislike.

"What do you recommend?" MacTavish asked.

"Perhaps," he paused . . . "Château Laville Haut-Brion," and he looked deeply at MacTavish.

Ah-ha! "Perhaps," MacTavish said evenly, "Perrières Meursault."

"A bit excessive, wouldn't you say, sir?" Boris said a bit too smoothly.

"Of course, if the cellar doesn't permit it . . ."

"Your selection shall be served . . . sir." And Boris wheeled, stiff as a manikin, and went for the wine.

MacTavish turned to Natalya. "Where did you find him, in the Kiev Zoo?"

"An old family retainer," she said, and bent to the soup. It was delicious, and MacTavish was ravenous. When Boris brought the wine he hardly noticed, but having tasted it he began to work on it in earnest. Even with the generous helpings of soup, the wine rocketed around inside him, and he felt its comforting fingers.

A green salad came and MacTavish continued to drink the wine through it, to Boris's obvious disapproval. MacTavish knew there was no wine that could be enjoyed with a salad, but he drank it anyway, in a kind of abandon. He was ready to surrender to anything.

"About this job, Miss Vorshova?"

"Can't it wait until we've eaten, Mr. MacTavish?" And the *Escargots à la Bourguignonne* arrived. So did Boris.

"We will have," said MacTavish, beginning to enjoy himself, "Bâtard Montrachet." He thought Boris looked a bit annoyed. It was a wine to seize the back of the neck, a wine with authority. MacTavish set to a bit more seriously; this could end at any moment, and he could wake up on the floor of the How Far Inn with a tongue like the shoe leather from No-Squeak Chun's.

Tao was stocking the table with *pain ordinaire* and taking away dishes. MacTavish tried once or twice to talk with Natalya, but she turned off the conversation without being offensive about it, and MacTavish finally bent his energies to the meal, one he was not likely to forget.

Tao brought the main course and announced it in an accent that might have been manufactured on the spot, or up from Southeast Asia. "Voilà," he said, *"les Quenelles de Brochet à la Nantua."* It smelled heavenly, and MacTavish, began to feel rather full. Boris rumbled in and once again stood over MacTavish. MacTavish could feel him vibrating.

"Your wine, sir?"

"What's *your* choice?"

"Hermitage Blanc."

"We'll have Pouilly-Fuissé."

MacTavish turned back to the meal, dismissing Boris, whose jaws were clenching in a rather alarming manner. *Screw it.* The fish dumplings were so good MacTavish couldn't restrain himself. He began to talk about the meal in clanging superlatives. Natalya merely smiled and slipped in a word now and then. He couldn't help but notice how low, how lovely, her voice was. And its accent was charming. "What part of Russia are you from?" MacTavish asked, between bites.

"Moscow . . . we lived there a long time. My father was an engineer. Do you know Moscow?"

"No."

She began to talk of Russia, and while she talked he ate. Once he noticed she scarcely touched her food, and he was conscious of the amounts he was eating. But he kept going.

"Fromage," said Tao, and "Château Timberlay" said MacTavish. He wasn't sure what Boris said. There was more desultory conversation. *"Flan aux Raisins,"* said Tao. "Château

Doisy-Vedrines," said MacTavish, and Boris fairly bolted from the room.

By now the candles were low and the table, despite Tao's quick work, reflected the ravages of MacTavish's appetites. Natalya still looked charming, but a little strained. Mac-Tavish was beginning to hit his stride. By the time he was ordering cognac, Natalya had excused herself and Mac-Tavish found himself alone, sipping and staring into space. He felt if he had to move some part of his body would give way and it would all spill out.

In the kitchen, Natalya and Boris were in furious debate. "He's eaten and drunk everything in the place," Boris fumed. "And you don't know any more than you did."

"He's not the kind of man you rush. I will take care of him in my own way, my own time. Just do your part . . . and Boris, don't interfere, do you hear?"

Boris tried to stare her down, and failed. "It's been a very expensive evening, you know. We must show some results."

"Don't try to bully me, you ox. You know we're not paying for this. This isn't even our house. We broke in here when we found out the owners would be in Taipei for the weekend."

"Still . . ."

"Oh, shut up, Boris."

"Are you going to sleep with him?" asked Boris, no longer able to contain his real annoyance.

She stared at him. "Did you not tell me this was vital to us? Is this a whim? Am I a whore?"

"Sh-h-h-h-h . . ."

"Damn you!" she shouted, and they both heard Mac-Tavish's chair squeak on the dining floor. Frozen, they heard him walk to the door and push it open.

"I thought I heard a shout," he said. He squinted at them. "What's going on?"

"Nothing's going on," said Natalya. Boris glared.

"Well," said MacTavish, "if you ask me, there's something up. For one thing, this isn't your house unless you're the widow of some Arab prince. And Boris isn't a wine steward, 'cause he doesn't like to argue about it enough, and Tao isn't a servant because you never, never serve the *escargots* after the *salade*. Now, what the hell's going on?"

Natalya moved toward him. "I will explain it all to you in a little while," she said. "Perhaps another time, if you will see me again?"

"Sure," said MacTavish, "but do you really have a job for me, or is this some kind of a game we're all caught up in?"

Boris moved at last. His right hand went under his jacket and came out with a very large pistol. MacTavish stopped and stared at it. Boris turned to Natalya. "There will be no need for you to seduce him, my dear. We will proceed, but we will do it my way."

"I'd rather do it her way," said MacTavish.

"You are stupid, Boris," said Natalya.

"Yeah, Boris," said MacTavish, still watching the gun. "You're pretty dumb to think you can get away with this, whatever it is."

"We're taking a trip, MacTavish."

"Ho-ho."

"He's not joking," said Natalya. "We have quite a way to go together. I hope it will be as pleasant as possible."

"Where to?" he asked her, but it was Boris who answered: "Somewhere in the north of Thailand."

"Oh, shit," said MacTavish.

THE RIVER

Hoon quivered like an arrow on the deck of his junk, and let out a mighty oath, repeating it in the several languages of which he was master. The crew reacted in all of them, for Hoon was absolute monarch, with the power of life and death, and equally important, the power of deciding how to split the loot.

And he was mad. "You turtle's piss," he yelled. "Were you sleeping?"

The unfortunate lookout cringed in the bow of the junk. Where had that log come from? It had deflected the bow, caused the steersman to panic, and they had run aground again on the inevitable mudflat of the sweeping Mekong.

None of them liked being this far upriver anyway; they were deep-water sailors and felt the oppression of the river-banks hemming them in.

Hoon, unconcerned as always with danger, ignored the oppression and toyed with the idea of shooting the lookout. It would be a good example to these dung-heads, and it would be one less to split the booty with. If they found it. But then it didn't pay to create too much dissension in the crew.

55

"Once more," he roared, "and I will dismember you day by day, beginning with what you laughingly call a penis."

The lookout tried to blend into the wood of the junk.

"And you," Hoon swung on the steersman, "the first to go will be your eyes, since you obviously don't use them and wouldn't miss them . . . and then your hands, since you don't use them either, you elephant's ass." For emphasis, Hoon kicked the steersman in the stomach and watched as he threw up on the deck. "Clean it up," Hoon yelled. And immediately turned his attention to a more pressing problem.

They were far up the Mekong, farther up than he had ever been. They were on a strange junk, and Hoon longed for his *lorcha,* that beautiful marriage of European hull and Chinese lug sails which had taken him over so many sea miles and into so many adventures.

This abomination was little more than a *twaqo* or a *sampan.* It was flat-bottomed and gaily painted, but it was too damned small for his crew and it was hard to sail. But it was what there was, and when he had commandeered it, he had known there would be problems.

He strode forward to look at their situation. The bow was deep onto the mud flat, but that was easily remedied; they'd simply get a tow and get off. The real problem was that they did not know exactly where they were going, and all these peasant villages looked alike from the center of the river. Hoon knew all about villages like these, since he had grown up in one, the bastard son with a dozen different bloodlines coursing, and sometimes clashing, inside his tall and muscled frame. He had known poverty, learned cruelty, decided to disdain fear, and reached out for life with both greedy hands.

Now he was on the trail of a great treasure . . .

"Go ashore and find some men from that village we just passed. Tell them we require them to pull us off the flats. Bring ropes. Tell them I will reward them if they come quickly. If they do not, say that Hoon will level the village." He was reasonably confident that even in this upcountry village, they would have heard of Hoon the Pirate.

The errant lookout immediately leaped from the bow of the riverboat and went up to his knees in mud. With great sucking noises he pulled his legs up and out and fought through the viscous mud toward the village. Hoon sat back to wait. His crew, a mixture of nationalities, temperaments, and racial types, stretched out on deck and tried to sleep through the noonday heat. In the nearby jungle the hum of insects was a low if constant background noise and the boat creaked gently in the eddies of the river. Hoon found himself dozing.

He let his mind wander . . . He could not remember when he had not been a pirate, but he could remember having been hungry. His schooling was hit and miss, and took place mostly in Macau, sometimes in Hong Kong, and more specifically at close quarters with merchantmen and other pirates in the South China Sea. He knew the tides, the storm signals, the intricacies of sailing a ship. And he could handle men.

It was a knack; you either had it or you didn't. Hoon's secret was that he genuinely was a better man than most of the men he met, and he threw it out there for them to consider, a little scent of danger that he let them sniff before he told them what he wanted them to do. He was tall, solid, young and quick. His strange hazel eyes seldom missed a man's sly reach for a weapon. He could spot a sail on the horizon before any of his crew. He could be as cruel as any mandarin, or as forgiving as a brother—it depended on his mood.

Hoon knew himself. He had no identity crisis and he knew where he was going in life. The search for treasure and the hardships at sea, the intrigues ashore and the constant high pitch of his life were merely manifestations of his questing nature. He was an adventurer, one of the last. He was a pirate because it was the most adventurous life he could find. If he had found cost accounting more thrilling, Hoon would have been a C.P.A.

But he was a pirate, and the latest adventure would either

make them all rich or get them all killed, and that was the kind of situation which Hoon enjoyed most. After a while all the intrigues and all the planning came down to matters of luck and skill.

Luck and skill . . . He wondered where he would find the man he was looking for. In one of these obscure villages? Dead in the jungle somewhere? Hiding out across the river, in Laos? He would seek him out, get the treasure, and slip back down the Mekong and work his way back to the open sea.

First he had to find his man, and first he had to get farther upriver.

He stood and walked the length of the vessel, his soft boots making no sound on the deck. His crew watched him uneasily, sensing his impatience.

The treasure will be a great one. Hoon turned to spit over the side of the boat. *But it is important to enjoy the search for it too.* Suddenly he heard them coming through the jungle like a herd of donkeys. A moment later he saw the villagers, a scrawny lot but bearing ropes, led by that dung-eating lookout.

The dozen or so men struggled through the mud to the boat. At Hoon's command they fixed the lines to the stern, and positioning themselves on both sides, began to seesaw the boat out of the mud. It took only a few minutes.

With the boat safely out of the mudflat, Hoon barked again and the lines were loosed. He turned to the lookout, who was standing waist-deep in the water. "Stay here, with the villagers," he said. "We may need a man on shore, and I will know you are here."

"But . . ."

"Stay," Hoon said firmly. He turned to the villagers and threw them a handful of coins. "For your trouble," he said. "Take care of my representative here until I return for him."

The crew had moved with accustomed skill and now the boat started upriver again. Hoon leaned against the gunwales and stretched as the boat slid through the brown water of the river. There was a warm sun and a gentle breeze, and he watched how the sun dropped spears of light through the forest canopy, and how the fanlike leaves stirred softly in the midday quiet. Occasionally there was the sharp cry of some jungle bird, but the sun was friendly and the air was peaceful. He felt very calm and confident, and he began to whistle an old Portuguese air he had learned in Macau, and the boat moved slowly but steadily north by northwest, taking him ever closer to the treasure which he sought. It was good to be alive, and young, and a pirate.

HONOLULU

Henderson Farley stood in the midday heat that bounced off the concrete of Honolulu International Airport. There were no hula girls, no leis, no welcoming committee. There was a surly nisei trying to get him a cab, and there was the same kind of noise and confusion that surrounds any airport, and he was thoroughly upset by it all. He could see across the expanse of runway and watch the heat waves shimmer and disappear into the bluest of skies. In the distance was Diamond Head, looking brown from the summer dry spells, and he could hear the roar of traffic.

Once, long ago, he had come in to the old airport in Honolulu, a graceful frame structure of aged wood and happy Hawaiians in *muumuus* and *holokus*. There had been much laughter and a few bottles passing hands and the men in large planter's hats with feather hatbands, and the big *tutus* kissing everyone in sight, related or not, and the sound of Hawaiian music—good stuff, not the exported kind—contributing to the happy noises. But progress had caught up and the airport now wasn't much different from anyplace else, except that it was a bit warmer.

After what seemed an eternity of frustration he had his

bags from the revolving counter and the nisei had managed to get him a cab. As he settled back in the large taxi, Farley decided to take stock.

He had his orders, his passport, his visas. He had his cyanide pen which actually wrote when not spraying deadly poison. He had his electronic transmitter in the Swiss watch, and a tiny receiver in his Optimist lapel pin. His briefcase broke down and could be reassembled into a sniper's rifle and his bowler hat was edible, in case he was stranded somewhere. His two pieces of luggage could zip together and be blown up to make a raft, and his shirt contained extra yardage in the tail so that he could make a sail for the raft, if necessary. His bifocals could be reversed, focused, and made into binoculars. His belt buckle was a minicomputer and the belt itself lined with bills in large denominations and in half the currencies of Asia. His innocent-looking phrase book contained microdots of agents' telephone contacts in South Asia. His wallet actually was *plastique*, which would be ignited via fuses or electric charge, and contained enough explosive to blow up a small house. Any unauthorized persons thumbing through his passport would, unknown to them, get enough unseen dye on their fingers to glow in the dark for weeks before it wore off. The umbrella he carried was either a .44 caliber rifle or a .410 gauge shotgun, depending on how he wanted to load it, and the ammunition itself was contained in the battery pack of his electric razor, which doubled as an infrared light.

He felt confident, ready. And he hoped the briefing up at Camp Smith would be helpful.

He sat back to enjoy the ride. The cab sliced into the traffic along the H-1 Freeway and started winding up toward Camp Smith. To his left he could see the ships in Pearl Harbor, and see the new stadium. Off to his right were homes and greenery, with Honolulu stretching out beyond, all the way to Diamond Head.

At the gate a young black marine halted the cab, and a

moment later a navy lieutenant stuck his head in the window. He looked at Farley for a long moment, then without a word got into the cab, and the marine waved them through.

The lieutenant introduced himself to Farley as Lieutenant Smith. Farley nodded but did not speak, and the silence remained unbroken as the cab stopped, deposited them in front of a small frame shack close to the Officers' Club at the edge of a small field, and sped away. The navy officer gestured and Farley stepped into the shack.

It was a compact room, containing a few individual chairs, a coffee mess, and a large map of Asia which took up an entire wall. Standing in front of the map was a stocky man with a crew cut—a marine in civilian clothes or one hell of a militant civilian. The man did not introduce himself, but he looked closely at Farley's identification. Then he went into the briefing.

At one point in the briefing Farley burst into laughter, but was silenced by a cold glance. Later on, he found nothing amusing about it all. Still later he wondered how the hell he could get out of the assignment. And all the while the briefing officer talked humorlessly, in a flat and unemotional voice, and his eyes never left Farley's face.

". . . and that concludes my briefing."

Farley sat very still and thought desperately. He wondered if it were too late to get Viper out here instead of himself. As the silence lengthened he searched for something to say that would make sense.

He cleared his throat. He scratched his nose. He frowned and looked out the window, trying to appear deep in thought, but his mind was off exploring some awesome possibilties, chiefly that he might be in over his head and need help.

"I might need help." he said at last.

"Who did you have in mind?"

"Perhaps . . . my assistant, Addison. Or Mr. Coleman, uh, King Cobra."

The briefing officer glared at him in what Farley thought might be contempt. "Adder," he said, "is an enemy agent. He has been arrested, but not before he passed on your mission."

Farley bolted upright. "Arrested! Adder?"

"You got it."

While Farley pondered the briefer elaborated. "Addison was arrested in the process of discussing your mission with a third assistant secretary in a certain embassy in Washington. We can only assume he got the gist of it across to them. Coleman has been placed in charge of the Washington operations until your return. *If* you return.

"*If* I return?"

"Nobody said it would be easy."

"But Adder . . ."

"Yeah. The other side knows, all right. They'll be waiting for you, somewhere in Asia. You'll sure have to keep a tight asshole, Farley."

Farley drew himself up. "Fer-de-lance, to you, whoever you are."

"All the same, watch your ass out there." Farley thought it might be as close to friendliness as crew-cut would get to anyone. Except a dying man on the way to the gas chamber.

"Ah, well, I, uh, I'd better get going."

"Yeah," said the man. "But you can't get out of here until tomorrow, so you might as well enjoy the Islands for an evening. And don't worry—we'll be keeping an eye on you here." Farley nodded.

All the way out and down the hill from Camp Smith, all the way down the freeway and off onto the Punchbowl off-ramp, all the way down Kapiolani Boulevard and into Waikiki, Farley thought about the mission, and now and then Adder crept into his mind. The dirty bastard! And Coleman in charge of the operations! He'd have curtains in Farley's office. There'd be brandy Alexanders in place of his vodka, pink ladies where his scotch used to be. God knows

64

what the silly son of a bitch would do to his wine cellar. At least there would be someone at his hotel Farley could discuss it with, for he had managed, through diplomatic pouch, to smuggle Phineas into the Islands, and would take him on to Asia. With Phineas you knew where you stood. Stout fellow.

He holed up at the storied old Halekulani, on the beach, one of the last outposts in an increasingly concrete Waikiki. He had a bottle brought to his room and he shared it with Phineas. Later, after a bath and another drink or two, he sallied out into the streets of Waikiki, trying to get a foretaste of the cultural shock he expected in Asia. From his earlier visit to Honolulu, he knew he would be awash in a sea of cultures, and he hoped Honolulu would cure his jet lag and gear him up for the ordeal in Asia.

How much of an ordeal he hadn't suspected until the briefing. Ah well, was he not the deadly Fer-de-lance? Had he not been in training for eighteen years for this mission? *Don't think too much about that.*

He had one of the world's great dinners at The Third Floor, and a significant amount of after-dinner hilarity at some piano bar on Kuhio Avenue. Several times he looked for the shadow he knew he'd have, but saw nothing suspicious. Skirting two hookers and a young man trying to sell him hashish, Farley made his way back to the Halekulani and into bed, and eventually into a fitful sleep. He dreamed he was Sinbad, on an adventure in Asia. Phineas was a giant roc, slightly drunk, and the two of them were trying to rescue a golden princess from a bunch of bandits.

When he woke up the most realistic part of his dream had been the bandits.

By noon, head throbbing, Phineas muffled, and all his paraphernalia intact, Farley was en route to do battle in Asia. He was several hundred miles in the general direction of Guam before he began to feel like his old self.

"What the hell, I can handle it," he said, and was startled

when the elderly woman in the seat next to him replied testily, "You do and I'll call the stewardess."

"Stick it in your ear, you old crone," he said witheringly. Fer-de-lance was back.

BANGKOK

MacTavish sat and sipped his scotch and watched the lizards swallowing tiny insects on the net that separated the hotel from the life that flowed with the Chao Phraya River, in the heart of Bangkok. Beside him Natalya lounged, unaffected by the heat, sipping a vodka martini and being both decorative and pleasant. The only sour note was the giant Boris, who also sat at the table. Boris was drinking vodka, neat, and kept his right hand significantly under his jacket in a constant menace.

"You know, Boris," said MacTavish conversationally, "you are probably the biggest shit I've ever known." He took another pull at the scotch. "I've known some big ones, too."

"Tell us, Mr. MacTavish," said Natalya. She was smiling.

"Well," MacTavish began. "There was my high school football coach who wanted us to give up girls or football, and naturally we gave up football. There was a hardass city editor who yelled a lot. There was a D.I. that I had in boot camp at Pendleton, a guy we tried to kill later but he escaped in a Miller beer truck. There was a bureau chief in Singapore who couldn't write his own name but sure wanted to tell everyone else how to do it; we went on the first unauthorized strike in Singapore after Lee Kwan Yew decreed no more strikes.

"And let's see . . . there was an Italian newsman—*Il Tempo,* he worked for—that I had a fight with in McMurdo Sound, Antarctica. There was a *Los Angeles Times* executive that I invited to, uh, follow a course of biological improbability. There was a banker in Hilo, Hawaii . . ."

"Is there any place you haven't been?" Natalya asked, with a voice like a South Seas trade wind.

"Nope," said MacTavish.

"You are a bore," Boris said, quietly. "Let's eat dinner and get back to the rooms. We have a long journey coming up."

"How the hell would you know, Boris?" MacTavish asked. "If you knew what the hell you were doing you wouldn't need me, right? So don't order me around too much, you outhouse commissar."

"It will be a pleasure to kill you someday," Boris intoned.

"Christ," MacTavish said, getting hotter. "If you want to have it out right now, give Anna Karenina here your hardware and we'll see who's the better man."

"I wish we could," Boris said, meaning it.

"Yeah," jeered MacTavish, "your mother wore combat boots."

"Huh?"

"Never mind. It's too complicated for your simple mind."

Natalya broke in. "Please," she said, "let's have a nice dinner. We have to be together for a time, so let's make it fun and interesting."

"Who could refuse you?" MacTavish beamed at her.

"Tell us about yourself," she said. "What is your first name?"

MacTavish looked at her; he couldn't refuse her.

"Clarendon."

"What?" she asked.

"It's the name of a hotel in Christchurch, New Zealand. It's where I was conceived."

"That's charming," said Natalya. Boris yawned.

"My mother was a circus acrobat, on tour. My father was a merchant seaman from Scotland. They met in Wellington, got drunk together in Akaroa, and went to bed in Christchurch."

"And so what do your colleagues call you?"

"MacTavish. My signer goes out on copy as Mac MacTavish."

"I shall call you Mac," said Natalya. "Unless you prefer Clarendon."

"Mac is fine," he said hastily.

"Mac," she said.

McTavish looked away and watched the lizards hunting. He was afraid to look too deeply into those startling green eyes. They could complicate his life. The other complication was that perfect example of arrested development, Boris, who was waiting for the opportunity to kill him, but not before . . .

"Tell me again, Boris," said MacTavish, "just why I'm along."

"You know why."

"I want to hear it."

Boris stared for a few seconds. "You know up-country Thailand better than almost anyone else in the world. You know the geography, the people . . . you know your way around. Very soon a lot of strangers are going to converge on a little village that sits in a curve of the Mekong River, across from Laos. We are all after the same thing. But you will give us the edge. You will help us get it."

"But what the hell is it?" asked MacTavish, remembering that this was where their talks had stalled earlier.

"We have nothing further to discuss. You will take us there, you will help us out, then we will go our separate ways."

"How did *you* know that *I* know what I'm doing up there?" MacTavish asked. "How did you get onto me?"

"A story—rather a series of stories—you wrote a year ago, for Reuters."

"And?" asked MacTavish.

Natalya leaned forward, and MacTavish got a good enough look to know she wasn't wearing a bra. "The way Boris explained it to me," she said, "was that the series indicated such a knowledge of the area that you were marked from that moment as an area specialist—someone we could use someday, if the need arose."

"So what's the need?"

"We're looking for something," Natalya said.

"Shut up," said Boris.

"And I'm supposed to help you? First of all, I don't work free; that's against my principles. Secondly, I may not know as much as you think I do, which is likely. Thirdly, I'm not a rabid flag-waver, but I sure as hell ain't procommunist, either. What makes you think I'll go through with it?"

"I'll shoot you if you don't," Boris said easily.

MacTavish regarded the two of them. Then he looked at Natalya. "is there any other kind of reward if I do my job?" He hoped she got the message.

"You're not too subtle, Mac," she said. "But we'll see."

Boris glared. "None of that," he said, including both of them in his frown.

"Let's order," said Natalya. Boris grunted. MacTavish studied the menu. How the hell was *this* one going to turn out. He could barely remember the Reuters pieces; hell, he couldn't remember all he should about the upcountry, either. Maybe it would come to him. Maybe not.

He thought about upcountry. It was one the strangest places in the world, yet it was explainable in Asian terms. Parts of it were nothing more than patchworks of poor acres, just subsistence farming. Other places were lush, wild, and wet. It was populated by snakes—cobras and kraits—and by assorted animals, including rare tigers and wild elephants. Often the elephants were tamed and used in the logging operations. To outsiders it would appear contradictory, a kaleidoscope of poverty and riches, barrenness and fecundity. To Asians, it made sense when you figured how far it was to marketplaces, how often the rivers flooded, who could get his hands on a gun, or the attractiveness of the village women. They measured by different clocks, upcountry.

During dinner MacTavish studied Boris, looking for a flaw in the defenses. Boris was huge, tough, watchful, and smart. He was also crammed with Marxist buzzwords, contempt for capitalism, and disdain for anyone who couldn't press his own weight. Watching Boris could be depressing.

Natalya was a different story. He watched her eat, a healthy girl who obviously took good care of herself. To see her alongside the Russian peasant women, quilted in fat, was like viewing a yacht moored beside a garbage scow. And, he reminded himself, she knew what this little excursion was all about, just as Boris did. Since Boris wasn't going to talk, maybe she would, if he could get her alone. But then they might not talk at all, heh-heh.

At that moment MacTavish caught sight of Sidney Stratton. There was a mild commotion at the entrance and considerable bowing and scraping. The television journalist entered in much the same way Caesar entered the Forum, and heads in the hotel restaurant snapped around for a better look. They saw a distinguished man in a dark blue suit and regimental tie, a man with glossy shoes and hair, a man impervious to the Bangkok heat, flies, mosquitoes, and cooking-charcoal smell.

"It is Stratton, isn't it?" asked Natalya. "I've seen him on television. He's so *handsome.*"

"It's Stratton," MacTavish confirmed. "At first I thought it was Napoleon. But no, it's Stratton all right."

"Who is he?" asked Boris.

"An American journalist, a television reporter," said Natalya.

"Do not call him a reporter as long as I am alive," MacTavish intoned. "We are not of the same breed."

"You are not," said Boris, "of the same class."

Stratton had taken a table after some discussion with the maitre d', who had wanted to seat him in the center of the room. With a great deal of false modesty he had selected a table with a better view of the river, and was perusing the menu with a slight scowl on his remarkably chiseled features. Occasionally he glanced up, satisfied that he was being watched, and went back to the menu. Waiters orbited him nervously.

At last the great man ordered, and sat back to await the service. As a succession of sommeliers and waiters were drawn into his gravitational pull, MacTavish began to hatch an idea. The longer Stratton sat there, the more MacTavish thought about it. The more he thought about it, the sillier it became, *but it might work.* Besides, it was time Stratton found out how the other half lived.

The moment came. MacTavish stood up. Boris's hand flashed under his jacket. "You fool," he hissed, "I will have to kill you if you move."

"I'm not moving, commissar," MacTavish said. "At least not yet."

"Sit down, please," Natalya begged.

"Or I'll shoot you, you idiot," Boris explained.

"Hey, Sidney!" MacTavish yelled.

There was a deathly quiet in the restaurant, and all motion stopped. Stratton moved his leonine head almost imperceptibly, aware of the sudden silence of the room and the moment of drama. His eyes slid around and he caught sight of MacTavish, standing, hands on hips, and grinning at him.

"Come join us, Sidney," MacTavish yelled. Stratton was shocked. Join *them!* He shook his head in dismissal, expecting instant obedience. To his chagrin he heard the upstart print reporter shouting again.

"Christ's *sake,* Sidney, unbend a little."

Stratton noted some agitation at their table, an angry shuffling by a large, bald and bearded man, and an effort to calm him by an extraordinary woman. By God, she was a beauty!

Where had he seen her before? He stood and began to walk toward them. Ah, well, it was good to descend from time to time and see what ordinary people were thinking. She *was* stunning.

Stratton went to the table with an air of benevolence. The upstart MacTavish he had seen once or twice, but the others were not known to him. As he approached MacTavish actually put out his hand. Stratton took it distastefully and turned his attentions immediately to the woman.

"Ah, how nice to see you," he mumbled, momentarily startled by the deep green of her eyes and the delicious curve of her breasts and shoulders and the deep glints in her hair, and. . .

"Natalya, Boris, this is Sidney Stratton," MacTavish was saying.

Stratton sat, never taking his eyes off Natalya. What a name! "Are you a famous ballerina, my dear?" he asked, and was rewarded with a flutter of long lashes.

"I think you should probably run along, Mr. Stratton," Boris said evenly.

Stratton turned, frowning. "What did you say?"

MacTavish leaned forward, hastily. "He's carrying a large gun, Sidney, my boy. He's virtually kidnapped me. We're going upcountry, to look for something. He's forcing me to come along. And now," MacTavish concluded, grinning, "he's forcing you, too."

Stratton was speechless, possibly for the first time in his life. Natalya broke the silence. "I am sorry, Mr. Stratton. I did not know this was going to happen."

Stratton looked deep into her extraordinary eyes. "Is this true?" he croaked.

"I'm afraid so," Boris said. "Your *friend*, MacTavish, has just gotten you involved. Quite involved. And I am quite angry. If anyone moves at this point, I will shoot."

"You son of a bitch," Stratton said, genuinely shocked. A moment later he swung on MacTavish. "*You* son of a bitch," he said. "You knew what you were doing. Why did you have to do this to me?"

"The more the merrier," said MacTavish. "And the better our chances of getting away from this maniac with the cannon. See anyone else in the restaurant you want to call over?" Boris leaned over and pressed his fork into the top of MacTavish's hand and began to push. MacTavish gasped.

"Once more," Boris said, "and you don't walk out of here alive."

"Christ, Boris," said MacTavish, "have you lost your sense of humor?"

"We leave now," Boris said, and dropped bills on the table. A wretched restaurant staff watched the great man and his new friends move out of the restaurant.

Their hotel lay in the general direction of the Wat Arun, the Temple of Dawn. They rolled in a small cab, Stratton bitching, across the river and through the lively streets of Bangkok. MacTavish actually got caught up in the scenery; it had been several years since he had seen Bangkok. He remembered getting drunk somewhere on Pat Pong Road, near the UPI office, eating in a Japanese restaurant, drinking still later in the classy bar of the Oriental, and buying Thai silk for some girl who claimed she was French and a chambermaid in the Hotel Normandy in Paris. He always wondered about that. Whether she was really French.

"Such a good town," MacTavish said, to no one in particular.

"You bastard," Stratton said.

Inside the hotel room Stratton launched into a spirited discussion of MacTavish's ancestry, and got around to including Boris. Boris waved the gun, and won silence. Later, Stratton was forced to call his own hotel and have his things sent over. He assured the clerk his network would pay the charges if a bill were forwarded.

"What about my cameraman?" Stratton asked. "I don't travel without him." But in the end, in a strained conversation, the cameraman was told to make his way back to Hong Kong and await further instructions. When he put the receiver back down, Stratton knew the umbilical cord had been severed, and he began to feel stirrings of genuine fear.

"What the hell are you doing in Bangkok, anyway?" MacTavish asked.

"On a story, of course."

"The royal fashions, I suppose. What the King and Queen are wearing these days. A new medal for the Field Marshal? Some ball-buster like that, huh?" Stratton tried to ignore him.

"What trappings the royal elephants are wearing? Where the Queen buys her star sapphires?"

Stratton whirled, stung. "A story that you couldn't handle, MacTavish. A story my network *assigned*, by God! Intrigue and thievery, and all sorts of international complications. Out of your league, entirely." Stratton sniffed at MacTavish and felt better. "Entirely."

"How you gonna do it without the big-eyed camera," MacTavish needled.

"I'll . . . I'll take notes."

"No notes," said Boris.

"I'll find a way to do the story, you ink-stained clod," Stratton said.

MacTavish sat and mulled it over. He was almost sorry for involving Stratton, but it made sense at the time. He would rope in others if he could. Safety in numbers. Boris couldn't watch all of them, all of the time. Deep in MacTavish's genes the latent ferocity of a Highland laird was stirring to life; there would be a way out of this, somewhere, and when the time came he wouldn't just walk away. *I'll find out what that Russian gorilla is up to, by Jesus Christ, by Ernest Hemingway, by Joe Namath. I'll find out and I'll feed it back in his teeth.*

Natalya stirred and six eyes clicked in focus. She stood up and stretched, lifting the short silk dress higher on her splendid legs. "I'm going to bed," she announced, and salacious thoughts surfaced like undersea missiles fired from a submarine. They watched her leave the room.

"Ah," said MacTavish.

"Um," said Stratton.

"Shut up," said Boris.

MANILA

He was a small, innocuous-looking man in a ridiculous bowler, carrying a briefcase and an umbrella, but when he stepped down at Clark Air Force Base near Manila, he got a royal welcome. The Air Force officers took him immediately to VIP quarters, and his bags were carried by no less than a bird colonel. That night he dined alone in his quarters, with a guard outside his door. The base officers wondered about him, but knew enough not to ask questions.

The next day the strange little visitor asked for a package of birdseed, a James Bond novel, and a bottle of Clos de Vougeot, and got them all. There were some raised eyebrows, but no questions.

And soon the little man was on a special flight out of Clark—a training flight which just coincidentally was flown by the best damned pilot based at Clark—and shortly was slipping in a silver dart over the broad, green, brown, sprawling, dirty, fascinating, lively, and turbulent peninsula of Southeast Asia.

As they approached Bangkok's Don Muang airport, the little man sat very still and thought about his briefing. Finally, he smiled, a slight, shy smile. The deadly Fer-de-lance was about to strike.

BANGKOK

Boris read the message for a second time. It had been so difficult to receive through their Bangkok Station (the KGB *rezident* was an idiot, Boris decided, which didn't smooth the receipt of such a long message) that he had hoped it was worth the trouble they had gone to. It was. Boris sat so that MacTavish and Stratton could see the gun in his waistband, and he sat at a distance across the room from them, alternately glancing down at the paper and up at his prisoners. MacTavish was pacing; Stratton, after considerable bluster, was sitting on the couch and looking forlorn.

SENDER: Four Section, KGB. For: Bangkok Station, relay to Petrov. D/T Grp 6061215. All follows for Petrov only. Acknowledge and comply.
Comrade! We salute you.
Considerable strain has been placed on our Asian operations due to the perfidy of those narrow-minded chauvinists who insist on running their own country. As you may know, certain Army officers were collaborating with the imperialistic, capitalistic, and mischief-making Americans, and unfortunately one of those Army officers also was a minor employee of ours engaged in

very low-level activities strictly for the good of his country, of course. Because this man has the integrity and morals of an alley cat, we find ourselves in an embarrassing position.

Boris Ivanovich, a certain object has been stolen in Bangkok and transported upcountry; this much you know, and you know why it is valuable to us. What you may not know is that the American Intelligence services, who are sending a despicable spy to capture the same object, also confided in certain unsavory persons in various illicit operations in South Asia. Thus we warn you: you could be in a lot of traffic up there.

Obviously, the Americans are trying to delay everything until they can get a real operation mounted. The operative they are sending has had little in the way of operational experience. His code name is Fer-de-lance, in the event you are able to intercept correspondence. He will cause you little trouble. The other element involved is a certain criminal from Macau, a brigand who is called Hoon. He is dangerous and unscrupulous and must be eliminated if he hampers your success. If you can capture Hoon or Fer-de-lance, we will be in a position to trade them to the Americans for two or more of our innocent diplomats whom the frenzied Americans apprehended in violation of all international laws and diplomatic immunity. The diplomats were merely leaving messages in a tree, and the Americans are threatening them with twenty years in prison for littering.

If you are able to complete this assignment successfully we will consider a new duty station with greater challenges, such as Paris. If you fail, we will have no choice except to bring you home for further training. Do I make myself clear? It is either *ooo-la-la* or *dum-de-dum-dum*.

At all costs, recover the object and send it in its entirety to me via diplomatic pouch. Also, I would like four yards of dark red heavy-weight Thai silk, a few more of those lacquered rings, size six, and keep your eye out for a good buy on sapphires. If you can get more of the Iranian caviar, please send it as well. Boris Ivanovich, the photographs were wonderful! Some day you must send me some of the scenery, too.

It was signed by the chief of Four Section, and Boris took it very seriously. Paris! Or. . .

"See here," said Stratton, breaking out of his reverie, "How long do you think we're going to sit around here like this? Do you know who I am, how many people will be looking for me? This could lead to war." That sudden thought was rather pleasing.

Boris looked at them both, as if seeing them for the first time. These two, or at least MacTavish, would help him up-country, and then he would be out of here and in Paris . . . but where would Natalya be? Ah, well, some sacrifices were necessary in one's career. Maybe he could take her anyway. . .

Feeling a sudden sense of urgency, Boris stood and glared at them. "You will be happy to know we leave within the hour. All arrangements have been made. Now we must hurry."

"Wait a minute, pal," MacTavish said. "You got a helicopter in your back pocket? Otherwise it's a train to Korat and a jeep from there, and I don't think there are trains outta here this time of day." Boris's silence impacted all at once. "For Christ's sake, Boris! We aren't going all the way in the damned *jeep?*" Boris smiled.

MacTavish groaned.

"What's the problem, here?" Stratton wanted to know.

"In your long and distinguished career, Sidney, you probably never rode in a jeep," MacTavish said nastily.

"Of course I have," Stratton lied.

"Not like this. Not a hundred and fifty or sixty miles over roads that goddamned *deer* couldn't walk on." MacTavish flung himself down on the couch in disgust.

Boris was happy, and waved the pistol. "We go," he said.

Natalya came in from the adjoining room. She was wearing something tan and tropical, pants and a jacket. She was radiant. "So," she smiled, "shall we go?"

MacTavish nearly snarled. "Shall we go? Shall we go? This isn't a woodsy hike. Why all the way in a jeep anyway?"

"In case we're not alone," Boris said. "Now, make some moves."

Stratton sat, brooding. He hardly stirred without his cameraman.

"Move," Boris said again. And they moved.

The jeep was ancient and bore a few distinguished wrinkles. Mostly it merely looked as if it had given up long ago, but was still being pushed to the breaking point. It was an indeterminate color. At the slightest movement it would be a mechanical symphony. It was hard to imagine that it had ever been new and relatively quiet. Stratton eyed the jeep with distaste, but was waved into the back seat with Boris. Natalya took the wheel, and as MacTavish slid into the front seat Boris handed him a map. "I won't need it," MacTavish said. Something Boris had said kept playing around the edges of his brain. *In case we're not alone,* he had said.

They had gone only a few hundred yards when they had to stop and adjust the load in the trailer hooked to the jeep. The trailer contained their luggage and various items of camping gear. The jeep sang and moaned, set up a counterpoint, and offered a great, earthy, saxophone sound. The trailer bounced and bumped along behind them. With the possible exception of Natalya, they began to sweat in the deep humidity.

The sky was overcast, that high haze common in Southeast Asia. Along the road they passed imposing *wats* and wretched homes of the very poor. Tall, graceful Thai girls walked toward markets in the late afternoon. Once they might have heard distant thunder, but when they listened they couldn't hear it again. *Perhaps it's just the way we feel,* pondered MacTavish. *Everything seems ominous now that we're into it. Except her.* He glanced at her profile; she was driving carefully but with a kind of gaiety, too. Her mouth was open in a slight smile and he thought he could hear her humming from time to time.

"You like this, don't you?"

"It's an adventure," she smiled.

"Yeah," he said, "it's thrilling to think old Boris might get a chance to shoot us." She shot him a sympathetic glance, but was lost almost immediately in handling the jeep.

"Turn right," he said, and they moved out on the road that would lead them to Korat and on north, to some obscure village to seek God knows what. MacTavish turned to look at Stratton. One of the best-known television newsmen in the world was looking around like a tourist, seemingly absorbed in the scenery. MacTavish wondered what he was thinking. If anything. A few minutes later he had his answer: Stratton was snoring.

Natalya hit a bump and the jeep sounded like the final few minutes of *Aïda.* MacTavish looked at his watch and estimated they were making somewhere between fifteen and twenty miles per hour. He hunched down in his dirty bush jacket, squinted through the windscreen and wished he were back at the How Far Inn, drinking Scotch with Chow Fun and Fu Manchu Two. Where would it all end? *In case we're not alone. In case we're . . .*

And the jeep rolled, whistled, jostled, and piped its way into the oppressive early evening.

LANGLEY

The Deputy Director, Covert and Clandestine Activities, Central Intelligence Agency, drove rapidly away from CIA headquarters in Langley. As usual, he thought wistfully of the Aston-Martin that spies were supposed to drive; he was sick and tired of his ancient Studebaker but the Chief wanted them to be inconspicuous, and his salary wouldn't permit a snappy sports car anyway. Not as long as he kept a mistress as well. At least if he had to drive this old clunker, it was taking him to *her*.

He eased into a quieter, older section of Washington and parked the car near her apartment. It was almost dusk, and he decided to wait in the car until he could approach the house unseen. It was a case of discretion being the better part of valor; her landlord had a large, dyspeptic mongrel that had terrorized him more than once. The dog's bark alone sent other neighborhood dogs into hysteria. Even worse was when the dog tore his trousers or gnawed at his ankle. Once it had gotten him right in the ass as he went over the fence in an effort to escape. He had been forced to show a worldly Washington cop his CIA identification after they had stopped him on the other side of the fence.

It was nearly dark now, and he decided to light the pipe he had been trying to smoke ever since he read that Allan Dulles had been a pipe-smoker. He lit it, spilled a few ashes in his lap and cursed under his breath. Where would the damned dog be at this moment?

Finally he crept up to the gate of the fence and peeked inside. Nothing. He opened the gate and heard its loud, sudden squeak. He also heard the scramble of four feet as the dog launched itself from the small porch on the other side of the house. He made for her apartment door on a dead run, hearing the dog's paws and the beginning of a rumbling growl. Fortunately, she had heard it as well, and flung open the door. He roared into the apartment and stopped, panting, listening to the dog pull up short outside the door and whine in disappointment.

"Damn!" he said, with feeling. Then he turned to look at her.

She was wearing his favorite negligee and holding out her arms to him. "John," she breathed, in that husky voice and strange accent he loved. Instantly she was in his arms and as he shifted to take her weight, they toppled backward on the couch. "You impetuous darling," she said, kissing him.

He tugged at his jacket but she was in the way. "Off," he said, but she was kissing him again. He tried to push his trousers down and get his tie off at the same time; her weight was crushing his arm and he couldn't explain because his lips were sealed, literally. It took most of his strength to throw her bodily onto the floor.

"Damn!" he said again.

She stared up at him. "John, darling, are you all right?"

"Stay away from me for a few minutes," he said, pulling himself together. "I need a drink."

She got up in a fluid motion and moved to the bar in one corner of her apartment. The negligee hid nothing and promised everything. Ah, he was a fortunate man! As she mixed the drinks he got out of his jacket and tie and took off his shoes. It was good to be, er, home.

She brought his drink, half beer and half tomato juice.

"They call this a 'red rooster' in Canada," he had explained, but she still shuddered every time she mixed one for him. She sat with him on the couch and sipped her vodka over ice.

"Well, how was your day, darling?" she asked. He looked into her brown eyes and down at the dancer's figure and back to the warm eyes.

"I love your accent," he said. "Have I told you that?"

"A thousand times," she said.

"Always sounds kinda European to me," he said, sipping his drink.

"Darling, we've been all through that. Why don't you sit back and let me give you a massage?"

"All right. But no tickling."

She got him out of his clothes and began rubbing him.

"What's new at the office?"

"Not much. We engineered a coup. Miss Brumley lost a file. We found out that one guy we thought was an enemy agent, a guy we trailed all over South America, was an encyclopedia salesman. A real one. Can you believe that? Oh, yeah. I'm supposed to manage the CIA basketball team; our season opener is with an Amish team from Ohio. They wove their own uniforms."

"Sounds exciting, darling," she said. She slipped out of the negligee and he turned over and kissed the back of her neck as she snuggled backward against him. He kissed her again and heard a sudden ringing. He stared at the back of her neck for a moment, then realized it was the telephone.

She got up and walked to the bar and picked up the receiver. "Hello," she said, paused and turned to him. "It's for you."

"Me!"

They stared at each other. "You might as well talk to him," she said.

He walked to the bar and took the telephone. "Hello."

"Why are you whispering?" the voice boomed at him. "Everybody knows about your little affair." It was the Director.

"How?" he asked, involuntarily.

"When you tried to get her a job in the office, but she couldn't type," the Director explained. "Not that that's a big requirement for secretaries in Washington. We checked her out and found out you were, uh, supporting her. It's all right, John. That's not why I called."

"Well, what's up, Chief?"

"We've got a little problem, John. As you know we've had personnel problems, budget problems, everybody writing books. In short, we're a little tight operationally, if you know what I mean."

"Yes."

"You remember buying a suit recently?"

"No."

"John, think for a moment. A suit."

The Deputy Director racked his brain. "Sorry."

"A suit, for God's sake. S.U.I.T."

"Ah," said the Deputy Director. "Now I get it."

"Well, John, in that entire nest of snakes we sent one of them out to the east, remember?"

"Sure."

"Send the rest."

"Huh?"

"We haven't any good men to spare, so I want you to get down there and get them started out to help him. The people I was going to send out have other things to do."

"I'll get right on it."

"Send Peebles to brief them and get them started."

"Right."

"Do it tonight."

"Right." He rang off.

He turned to her. "I have to go."

She walked over and kissed him. "I understand, darling."

He got dressed and she slipped back into her negligee. At the door she kissed him lovingly and gently closed the door behind him.

She walked back to the telephone, reached behind the bar and turned off the tape recorder, smiling to herself. From outside she heard the scurry of feet and the sounds of a chase, following by a deep, satisfying growl and a sudden scream of pain. Then silence fell on that quiet section of Washington.

THE RIVER

Hoon ordered his junk moored to a make-shift dock beside a village that looked like all other villages, all bamboo and thatching and peasants. He decided to look it over; somewhere up here he had to start making noises, throw his weight around a little, see if he could stir up some information. What he had was meager, but it was a start, and he knew that once into it he would warm to the chase.

"No girls," he told the crew. "No house-burning for fun. No stealing, except for enough chickens for dinner. Get some rice, too. No shooting anybody. No burning the village in order to save it from anything. And remember, we aren't up here to make friends, just to get the treasure, so if anyone looks as if he knows something, get it out of him, or tell me about it."

They stepped from the junk onto the rough dock where the Mekong River boats tied up. In front of them was a steep bank with rickety wooden stairs, and they filed up it with Hoon in the lead. He wore jungle boots and cargo pants and what was left of a British officer's white mess jacket. He carried a World War II carbine and on his left forearm was the Malaysian throwing-knife no one had ever seen him without.

He took a dozen of the crew and walked down the path to the village. There was the usual office building, baked mud bricks, one story, square. In it, Hoon knew, would be an immigration official, perhaps the only person in the village who could read and write. He would also be the chief of the hamlet. Around the immigration shack would be dozens of homes, made of bamboo but neat and very functional for the jungle, except that there seemed to be no way to build a protection against the snakes.

As Hoon moved through the village it was as he expected. A few villagers came out to stand silently and stare at the newcomers, but most remained within their homes. Hoon could see large brown eyes watching him.

The crew began to disperse and gather dinner, the villagers watching without complaining. These newcomers were relatively well behaved. Hoon strolled through the village, noting the various trails out of it, weighing the village's prosperity as shown by the small gardens and neat houses. Not bad. He singled out a young boy standing near the entrance to one of the houses, and stopping in front of him, Hoon gave the boy a chance to look up at him, to see the fierce eyes and the carbine. "Where is your guru?" he demanded of the boy.

The boy looked up and his eyes flickered once. He understood he was being questioned, knew the word guru. He pointed. Hoon turned to look. The boy was pointing up one of the trails. He looked back and smiled at the boy and gave him a coin. The guru would know what he, Hoon, needed to know.

Hoon went up the trail, leaving the crew to keep an eye on the village. The trail was muddy. Water still dripped from the broad leaves, and the tall bamboo clacked together in the slight breeze. The rains were unpredictable; but when they came, even for an hour a day, they were bone-drenching. Hoon walked carefully, watching the bushes alongside the trail.

He came to a shack. It had a small terrace, and on it, an old man was sitting and watching him approach. Hoon walked straight up and without invitation, sat on the edge of the terrace. He studied the old man.

"What do they call you?" he asked the old man.

"They do not call me," said the old man. "It is I who call them."

"And what do you call them?" Hoon was amused.

"Whatever I think of," said the old man, honestly.

"I seek information," said Hoon, driving to the point.

"Yes. Otherwise you would have asked questions in the village."

"Huh?"

"Never mind. What is it you seek?"

"I want to know of a man," Hoon began. "He would be a young man, and in great danger. He would be coming from the south, carrying something. He might have passed through this village. Again, he might not. What can you tell me?"

"I can tell you that to seek material things is a waste of a life." Hoon waited.

"I can tell you that when you dine with a tiger the tiger dines last." A few moments went by.

"I can tell you that the best things in life are free."

Hoon pulled out another coin and laid it carefully on the mat in front of the guru. The guru stared off in space. "Such a one as you describe . . ."

Hoon waited expectantly.

". . . did not pass this way. *But,* I have heard that upriver past Borabue, past Maha Sarakham, there is a guru who knows all there is to know, as he was once a resident of Bangkok."

"Do you know the name of the village?"

"It has no name.'

"And the guru?"

"He is called the Old One."

"Can they be reached by river?"

"The village can. The Old One can be reached only by a spiritual pilgrimage."

"Tell me," said Hoon. "Do you gurus have a union?" The guru's smile was enigmatic.

Down the trail and into the village again, Hoon began to round up his crew. He moved them quickly toward the waiting junk.

As they cast off, Hoon barked the command that would take them upriver, and immediately felt a quick thrill of pride. Any other crew would have balked; they were out of their element already, being this far inland and linked to the fixed course of the river. But this crew obeyed with alacrity.

"We are after great treasure," he told them. For the hundreth time, he wished he knew exactly *what* the treasure was. The only thing he knew for sure was that the American who had told him about it was trustworthy, and had said it was a fabulous fortune. "It would be," said the American, "at least ten times as much as a good rock group makes in a year."

Later, squatting on deck and eating the rice and chicken, slightly apart from the crew, Hoon felt better than ever about the adventure; he began to feel they were closing in. Now to find the Old One. . .

THE JUNGLE

Thanat, the immigration officer, sat back in his chair and looked straight out the window at Laos, across the river. All around him the life of the village ebbed and flowed, leaving little streams of humanity in motion outside his door. Sometimes there was driftwood as well, the old beggars who seemed to have washed up here on the rim of the river. He tried to shut his mind to the incessant noise of the village at midmorning, but the sounds kept infiltrating.

The colors, too, breached his defenses. The jungle was closed and constant, a world of greens and browns, myriad and interesting hues, clamoring for attention by their intensity. He hated the jungle. He hated the village, too. Mostly he hated being here, in this sweltering, squalid peasant's world, without movies or amplified music. He was still young and married to a pretty wife who had begun to nag: Why are we in this world of peasants? Who did you not bribe that we would end up here, so far from Krung Thep or Udon or any other city where there were things worth doing and seeing? Why are we stuck out here? Have you no future?

No future.

His daily routine was simple; he would roll from atop his pretty wife and watch contentedly as she prepared breakfast. He would get to the office early, before the heat set in. He would stamp passports and paste the pink stamps in the passports of foreigners who occasionally passed through en route to Laos, or he would stamp them again as the returning foreigners pushed their passports at him across his mostly-bare wooden desk. He wondered, but he did not ask, what so many foreigners were doing in Laos. He had been there once, and found it almost exactly like northeast Thailand. Even the language was the same in most villages.

Before noon he would lock the doors and go home again where his wife would be preparing a simple meal. He would eat sparingly because of the heat, then take a nap. Sometimes he simply stayed home, but if he sensed there would be traffic across the river he would go back to the office and wait.

The magazines in his office were years old, and in several different languages. There were no books in the village. There was an ample supply of beer, though, and he noticed a slight pot developing after a few months on the job. There was little else to do, except drink beer and mount his wife. He longed for the excitement of the nightclubs, where the music was loud, loud, and the round, revolving chandelier threw miniature stars around the room, and the girls were tender, for a price.

He sighed. There was so little to do here. As he had more times than he wanted to count, Thanat sat back in the rickety wooden chair and stared at the green border just beyond the mud of the river bank. *The river.* He should be on it, in a houseboat, with a Swedish actress, one he could fall into like dropping into a great, white, enveloping cloud.

And then he heard the noise. It seemed to be all about him, bouncing from the very earth, setting up hysteria in the village dogs and rattling the office where he sat. He bolted upright and ran to the door and looked up. It was a helicopter, the first he had ever seen.

96

He ran out onto the grass in front of the office. The few villagers he saw were transfixed and staring. Thanat felt a little thrill of superiority: at least he knew what it was, he had seen pictures. He had no idea it could be so noisy, and he wondered if it were amplified, like the guitars in the nightclubs.

It was coming down. As he stood, gaping, the helicopter descended ever so slowly. Thanat could see the white face of the pilot, and feel the beat of the moving wings. The helicopter settled gently on the grass and a door slid back. A figure climbed out, rather awkwardly, and ran in a crouch under the still-turning blades. Thanat tore his attention away from the figure as the helicopter suddenly began to lift again, making even more noise than before. Dust blew everywhere and Thanat cursed and closed his eyes. When he opened them again the dust was settling and the helicopter was pulling up, gathering speed, and moving to the south.

He looked at the approaching figure. It was a foreigner, all right, but no taller than himself. The man was dressed in khaki shorts, khaki bush jacket, knee socks, boots and what Thanat, having seen several old movies of White Hunters in Darkest Africa, finally determined was a pith helmet. On the man's shoulders sat a large and evil-looking parrot, its feathers ruffled and its throat emitting a series of low grumbles.

As the man neared Thanat could see he wore glasses with somewhat thick lenses. Over one shoulder was slung what appeared to be a first-aid kit; over the other was a carrying case of some kind, contents unknown. The man was carrying a duffel bag with one hand and as he neared Thanat, he was wiping his forehead with the handkerchief he held in the other. Thanat watched, spellbound, as the exotic figure walked straight up to him and stopped. Thanat still stared as the man put down the duffel bag and held up one hand, palm out.

"How," he said.

"How do you do, Mr. Hao . . . or Hau. Is that with an 'o' or a 'u'?"

The man beamed at him. "You speak English!"

"Sure," said Thanat. "I speak it well, I am told."

"Sure you do. Well, that helps." The man took off his glasses and began polishing them with the handkerchief, looking around at the villagers who were standing, rooted, and watching the stranger.

"What can I do for you, Mr. Hao?"

"Not my name. Can we go inside?"

Thanat gestured, then followed the stranger inside the office, where the stranger promptly swung one plump leg over the corner of Thanat's desk and made himself comfortable. The parrot shifted and started quarreling again.

Thanat walked around and sat behind his desk, his mind whipping back and forth. The newcomer certainly was one of the strangest visitors *this* place had ever seen. As Thanat looked up his peripheral vision caught several of the villagers staring in through the open windows. Thanat put on his best official mask and said, almost brusquely, "Now then."

The visitor adjusted his glasses and, still sitting, reached in one pocket of his bush jacket and produced a passport. He put it on the desk where Thanat looked at it for a moment, then reached forward and opened it. He looked at the name.

"You are J. Bonde?"

The little man took off his pith helmet. "Right," he said.

Thanat looked down again. And looked up. "Your occupation?"

"I am a zoologist."

Thanat considered it. "And why are you here, Mr. Bonde?"

"I am looking for birds and animals. For a zoo."

Thanat sat back in his chair. "And what do you need from Immigration?"

"A stamp. In my passport."

"So?"

"So I can work on both sides of the river, here and in Laos. Your government has given me a free hand, as you will see in the letter inside the back, there."

It was true. The government promised all assistance. All Thanat had to do was stamp the passport, and J. Bonde could go over to Laos as necessary. Over there, of course, he might have a whole different set of problems, but that was his worry. Thanat appeared suddenly busy, in the practiced way of bureaucrats everywhere. He shuffled in his seat and rocked slightly back and forth, sniffing and pushing gently at the passport. Finally, he stamped it and handed it up to the man who sat watching him with growing impatience.

"Thank you," said Bonde.

Thanat nodded, expecting the visitor to make his departure. Instead Bonde pushed his pith helmet back on his head and peered at Thanat. "I'll also need a boat, to go up and down the river," he said.

Thanat glanced down at the wristwatch he had bought long ago in Bangkok. "That is impossible at the moment. You will have to return this afternoon."

"This afternoon!"

"Yes."

"But I'm in a hurry."

"No one is in a hurry here."

"I must have a boat."

"You must wait until this afternoon."

They stood, glaring. Finally Bonde reached in yet another pocket and pulled out a large wallet. Deliberately, he peeled off several bills and laid them on the desk. Thanat looked around; the villagers were still there. Now he *had* to take the bribe, or the villagers would consider him a fool. He reached down, picked up the money and counted it. A goodly sum. He stuffed the bills in his pocket. "This afternoon," he said, and began to move for the door.

Outraged, Bonde followed him outside.

"But you took the money!"

"This afternoon, Mr. Bonde," he said, moving away. The pretty wife, the noon meal, and a nice nap were waiting for him.

As he walked quickly away from the office the little man

pranced after him. "But you took the money," he said again, his voice a little higher. "It's dishonest! Not to go through with a bribe!"

"Remember your Kipling, Mr. Bonde?"

"What?"

"I don't know it exactly, but it's something about a fool lies here who tried to hustle the East. I'll see you here this afternoon. We'll get you a boat then. There is one store in the village, down the path there. It sells 33 Beer from Vietnam, or Tiger Beer, all made with good Mekong River water. I suggest you have a drink while you wait."

The parrot screamed suddenly. "And one for your bird, perhaps?" Thanat said.

Watching the upstart Immigration officer walk away from him, Farley fairly shook with anger. Time was precious; time was vital. He had to find the right village, pick up the trail of the thief and run him to ground.

He didn't know how much time he had. Or how much opposition was mounted against him.

"Shit, shit," he said, and went off to find the village store.

The wait seemed interminable. He sat on rickety steps in front of the store, drinking beer and pouring an occasional shot for Phineas to drink from the bottom of his pith helmet. All the time the villagers sat watching him. *Look at them stare. You'd think they were watching the Vikings and the Rams.* He kept glancing at his wristwatch. He could feel the sweat forming a watercourse around various humps and mounds of his body, working its way finally down his backsides and into his crotch. He could see the heat haze from the barren places the jungle had yet to claim, and if he strained he could hear the gentle lapping of the river water against the bleached wooden pier. He tried not to strain, for he knew that Fer-de-lance would need all his strength and cunning in this alien world. It was strange, but what he wanted most at the moment was a glass of milk. He took another beer instead.

Still later, with a slight headache digging in for the evening, he saw the Immigration officer stroll back toward the office. He got up, and calming Phineas, walked back to the office to find Thanat talking with one of the villagers, a middle-aged man in dirty pants and shirt and a white stubble of beard, like scrub grass in winter.

"This man will take you up and down the river as you wish, Mr. Bonde. You see, it is not complicated."

"How much?"

"Fifty *tical* a day. He has no family, you see, and can work cheap."

Fer-de-lance pretended to consider. He really didn't know if that were cheap or not, but time was pressing. There would be many villages to visit. "Are most of the villages up here along the river?"

"Yes," said Thanat, surprised. "It is the best farming area. Of course there are poor villages all over the countryside, but most try to gather near the water routes. Why do you ask?"

"For supplies, if need be."

"I see," said Thanat. *If J. Bonde eats the village food, he will spend the next week squatting. But that's not my problem. It's his.*

It was a short walk to the pier. The boatman stepped aboard a small, flat-bottomed sampan, no more than twenty feet long. The boatman pushed them away from the pier and began to pole them out into the center of the river.

Thanat watched them go with a slight twinge of guilt. After all, Bonde *did* have a letter from the government in Bangkok, so perhaps it wasn't nice to send him off with the village idiot in his notoriously leaky boat. But then, he shouldn't have been so . . . so . . . *strange* either.

Thanat leaned back in his chair and gazed at Laos, across the river. He wished his pretty wife would quit nagging him, but he had to agree with her. It would be more exciting in one of the cities. Nothing ever happened in this up-country border town.

MacTavish sat, full of Spam and rice and black coffee, and watched the fire dwindling. It was a warm night, and he wondered how many snakes were making a pilgrimage toward his sleeping bag. He wondered how he would defend himself against them with his hands and feet tied, for obviously that's what Boris, that great humanitarian, had in mind. Boris could not afford to stay awake all night.

Natalya sat on his right, the eighth wonder of the world. She had been all day in a bouncing jeep, driving most of the way in fact, and looked right now as if she had stepped out of a shower and were ready to face the day. How could she go through all that unwrinkled? The sun that had burned everyone else had turned her into something golden and shining, and she had kept her even disposition. She seemed to be having a good time.

On the other side of the fire sat Sidney Stratton. For most of the day he had seemed bewildered. Some of the time he had appeared on the verge of either crying or running amok. MacTavish would have welcomed either one.

Standing in front of the tent, Boris was sipping vodka from a thermos and dreaming of Paris. *Le can-can, white thighs with net stockings, silk underwear. Or cold faces and gray winters, deep cold and unheated apartments. Better to think of French girls and good champagne and Parisian nights. Boat trips on the Seine . . .*

"Hey, Boris." He looked up, annoyed.

"How do you know where to go from here?"

Boris did not like the question. "We will look around a little tomorrow."

"Meaning you don't know where you're going," MacTavish said.

"Meaning we will look around a little tomorrow."

"Listen, pal," MacTavish said, "I can take you anywhere up here you want to go, but I have to know where it is."

"You will know in good time."

"Like tomorrow?"

"I will tell you in good time," Boris almost shouted.

"Shit," said MacTavish, "I should have known you wouldn't know what you were doing."

"Don't provoke him, please," Natalya said suddenly.

"What do you care?" MacTavish asked.

"I care."

"Then you tell me where we're going."

"All right," she said calmly. "I will."

"No," said Boris.

Natalya turned to stare at him. "Why not? He has to know sooner or later."

"Right," said Stratton, stirring. "Sooner or later."

"The fact is," said Boris slowly, "she doesn't know where we are going."

"I can understand that," Stratton said, plaintively. "I don't even know where we've been."

"We are looking for a village," Natalya said suddenly. "But we don't know much more than that."

"Why not?" asked MacTavish.

"Because . . ."

"Enough," said Boris. "As we near it, I will tell you what you need to know."

"I think you'll do it now," MacTavish said easily, "or we don't go tomorrow. And don't give me a lot of crap. You need me up here, remember? So let's have it, or I don't answer reveille in the morning."

Boris reached in his waistband and pulled the large gun again. He pointed it straight at Sidney Stratton. "And if you do not," he said, "I will shoot your colleague between the eyes."

"My God," Stratton yelled, "that would disfigure me! I'd lose my job!"

Boris laughed, put the gun away and took another pull at the vodka. MacTavish had turned away and was looking beyond the firelight. "I would hate to deprive journalism of the great contributions made by His Eminence."

"Why thank you, MacTavish," Stratton said, pleased.

MacTavish's worst fears were confirmed; Boris tied them expertly and left them side by side in the sleeping bags. Natalya had the tent along with the gear, and Boris, with extravagant gestures, placed his bag in front of the tent.

It was one of the worst nights of MacTavish's life. Stratton was asleep immediately, the deep, noisy sleep of the innocent or the vacant. Natalya was just yards away, undressing on the other side of that thin sheet of waterproof nylon. Now she was taking off her shirt . . . now her bra, now . . . that way madness lies. After a while he stirred and tried to pull at the leather thongs around his wrists. Boris was instantly awake and MacTavish knew it was as he feared it would be: Boris was the compleat watchdog, and a light sleeper.

He lay back and looked up at the sky. With the dying down of the fire he could see the stars more clearly. He remembered the first few trips he had made up here, with some American army units trying to learn what they could about jungle fighting. It was a long time ago. He had come again and again to this part of Thailand because he admired the people and because it was a true place. The problems were real, and the rewards were great for an enterprising reporter. He had written a lot of good stuff then. A long time ago . . .

He began to doze, with Stratton snoring in his ear. In a few minutes he had to turn, looking for a better position. It went on like that most of the night, and by the time Boris was shaking him awake, with the sun already heating up, Natalya was dressing in the tent, Stratton was sitting up and seemingly rested, Boris was actually whistling, and he, Mac-Tavish, felt as if he had spent the night making love to a rock crusher.

They were on the road again in less than an hour, Mac-Tavish glad to have his wrists and ankles operative again, but alarmed at the ferocity of Boris's coffee, which lingered in his mouth and made him long for a soothing belt of scotch.

For the next hour MacTavish tried to doze in the front seat. Once he stirred and looked around; so far they could have made the trip without him, for the road, although full of potholes, was well marked. The real navigation would come much later in the day. Meanwhile, Natalya handled the jeep well, but not expertly, and they crawled along the rutted road through scrub trees and high grass.

Shortly before noon they came into a more forested area, which MacTavish recognized. From here the jungle would get thicker until they hit the heavy wooded areas which marked the sawmill country of the north, while the eastern sector flattened out into the scrub trees and farmland areas that stretched on to the Mekong, and beyond the Mekong was Cambodia.

MacTavish was thinking of Cambodia when the snake dropped into the jeep.

It fell from an overhanging tree branch and landed heavily on the windscreen. There was a split second of frozen silence before everyone reacted in four distinct variations of panic:

Boris whipped out the gun and fired wildly.

Natalya screamed and arched back in the seat, taking her hands off the wheel.

MacTavish dived headfirst out of the jeep.

Stratton stood, as if to say something, and fell backwards out of the jeep. As he lay face down in the dirt, the trailer made two wheeltracks across the back of his expensive bushjacket.

Meanwhile the snake, untouched by any of Boris's several shots, slithered onto the floor of the jeep while heavy-caliber slugs exploded through the glass of the windscreen and tore through the floor of the jeep. Others ricocheted off various metal parts of the vehicle and caused Natalya to scream again, this time at Boris, although never taking her eyes off the bewildered snake.

Then the jeep lurched into a tree. Natalya was thrown forward against the steering wheel, but bounced back. Boris, who had crouched to fire at the snake, soared over the front seats and crashed onto the hood, then slid to the ground where he lay, dazed. The snake hurried over the back seat of the jeep and dropped gratefully to the ground, heading for the nearest cover.

For more than a minute there was silence except for the various strange noises coming from the jeep, whose engine had stalled but whose *corpus* continued to wheeze, groan, hum, and buzz. Somewhere in its entrails there was a wet, gurgling sound.

Boris raised himself on his elbows, still holding the gun. He moved experimentally and found everything responsive. He sat up slowly, his head still full of fog. There was Natalya, getting out of the jeep now and obviously unhurt. And there was Stratton, also sitting, staring in disbelief at the dirt on his clothing. And MacTavish . . .

MacTavish was gone!

Boris bolted upright and looked quickly in a circle. No sign of him. The big Russian ran back down the road to the spot where the snake had dropped on them.

"MacTavish!"

Boris was furious. He swung in a circle, still holding the gun, then he began to trot through the nearest line of trees, zigzagging and looking for signs of MacTavish.

"You can't escape, MacTavish."

He crashed on through the woods, waving the gun and yelling. He began to pant. Sweat popped up and began to flow freely in the midday heat. The only sound he could hear was his own heavy running. After a while he stopped to rest, and think. Where could he be? He, Boris, was in pretty good shape and he had covered a lot of ground. MacTavish must be in better shape than he looked to get so far. Unless . . .

He wheeled and started to spring back in the direction he had come, hoping against hope. He heard the jeep start, heard the gears rake, heard the cacophony as the jeep was pushed to its limits in first gear. He broke out of the tree line in time to see the jeep flash by. MacTavish was driving. Stratton, in the back, was holding Natalya's arms behind her.

Boris risked one shot, afraid of hitting Natalya. In the boom of the gun he thought he heard the slug impact, but the jeep kept going and a thin film of dust floated in the air behind it. He allowed himself a moment, only a moment, to reflect on Paris. Then he turned and began to jog back down the road. He had to get another jeep and get after them before he lost the trail entirely.

The thoughts of what he would do to that dog's-meat reporter kept him going. The untrustworthy bastard. No wonder the Press was hated everywhere.

"Is she tied?"

"Yes," Stratton said.

"Sorry, my dear," MacTavish said over his shoulder. "We can't gamble on your loyalties." He was watching the road carefully, but he was exultant. "How about that, Stratton? You ever see anything like that?"

But Stratton was concerned with his own problems. What great footage this would make, himself in an open jeep with a beautiful woman, a beautiful *Russian* woman, in the wilds of northeast Thailand! Let them look at this in the Erawan bar, by God! Sidney Stratton, himself, great machismo stuff.

". . . enough Apache pictures."

"What?" Stratton asked.

"Old Boris," MacTavish said, gloating, "he hasn't seen enough John Wayne movies. That's always how you outwit the enemy . . . lead them away and double back."

"Boris will catch you," the girl said.

"In a pig's ass, he will," MacTavish retorted. "Nothing can stop us now."

At that moment the jeep went eerily silent, and a second later, rolled to a quiet end in the center of the road. Even before his feet hit the road, MacTavish knew it was hopeless.

"The jeep is dead," he said quietly, feeling the bitterness rise in him.

"Boris will catch you," Natalya said again.

"Now what?" Stratton was running his fingers through his hair.

MacTavish squinted to the north and south, trying to look like he knew what he was doing.

"If we try to go south, we'll bump against Boris the Bear-like. We'd better go north."

"What's wrong with east or west?" Stratton wanted to know. "It's a big country."

MacTavish rubbed the stubble on his chin. "East takes us to the Mekong River and Laos, where we either stop or go downriver into Cambodia. I don't like what's happening either place, so that's out. West takes us into very, very dense forests. We might find a village there, but it's a hell of a trek in the jungle, and I've had enough of the snakes for now. Natalya?"

"Yes. North. There's no other choice."

"But that means walking," Stratton said, horrified.

"Just until we hit a village. Then we'll hitch a ride on northward, cross the Mekong at Nong Khai and get into Vientiane and fly straight out to Hong Kong. Leave old Boris looking for us behind every tree in Thailand."

"But he might fly into Vientiane and work his way back down, looking for us," Stratton said.

MacTavish looked at Natalya. "Is he that bright?" She shrugged.

"Well, let's keep going north for a bit. Then, if we can work it out, we'll peel off into one of the villages and maybe go down the Mekong on a boat and double back by land to Bangkok to the southwest."

"Without the jeep," Natalya said, gloomily.

"Yeah."

Stratton sighed.

They pulled out the canteens, and stuffed their pockets with snacks from the trailer's food supplies. They turned north, and began to walk. Stratton mumbled something under his breath.

"What?"

"I sure could use my cameraman," he said. But already he was working on how to recreate this moment on a set. Gordon of Khartoum. Clive of India. Lawrence of Arabia. Stratton of the Jungle.

WASHINGTON

Ken Coleman, the King Cobra, had redone Farley's office, as Farley had feared. There were new curtains of an indeterminate pastel hue, and a wall adorned with large pictures of weight lifters in various poses. There hadn't been time to change the atrocious carpeting, but Cobra had found time to throw out all of Farley's macho James Bond novels. Farley had no taste. Cobra was particularly proud of the new, softer lighting. Now that they were active, the unit was able to get almost everything it had asked for.

One of the things he had asked for was a complete briefing on just what Farley was doing in Asia. Adder, that silly twit, had been unmasked at last and shown to be the horrendous creature Cobra had always known him to be. Adder had been taken away without any word to the staff and without any expression at all on his sallow face and he, Cobra, had felt no pity. Imagine, a double agent. Cobra shivered slightly.

A dry cough brought him back to reality, and he tried to focus his attention again on the man sitting in the imitation Hepplewhite chair Cobra had selected himself. He was a small man with a massive forehead and a quizzical squint.

He might have been an economics professor or an assistant city editor, but he was, in fact, *their* newly assigned liaison officer; *they* weren't going to let the unit languish for eighteen years again. So the liaison officer, whose name was Peebles, had come down to do the briefing, and had hardly started when he saw Cobra's mind wandering.

"If you're ready for me to continue . . ."

"Oh, yes," Cobra said, trying to charm Peebles. "Please."

"As I was saying . . ."

"Do go on. You brief divinely."

Peebles shifted and squinted at Cobra.

"Agent-in-charge Farley was sent to Asia to try to recover a stolen object before the opposition does. The reason he was sent is that frankly, the Agency was furious that your unit had not accomplished a mission in, uh, eighteen years. Also, most of the operatives we could have used in Asia are either known to the opposition or else they're indigenous personnel."

"What?"

"Natives."

"Oh."

"So we employed Farley, briefed him enroute, and he should be closing in on the target by now. Of course, since it was stolen and left in an up-country village, the problem becomes one of finding it, and doing so before the opposition does."

"Um," said Cobra.

"Complicating the problem is that the stolen object literally is priceless. We want it for what it contains, but it alone—its intrinsic value—is enough to draw every mercenary and thief within the hemisphere. But we don't care how much the object is worth. It's what it holds that makes it so valuable to us and to the other side."

"Dear boy, *who* is the other side?"

Peebles smiled. "How long have you been in this business?"

King Cobra smoldered. "At least eighteen years, as you must know."

"The other side," intoned Peebles, "is anyone who isn't *us.*"

"That's sweet," said Cobra.

"To continue. If we cannot obtain the stolen object through Farley, we have a secondary plan. We have leaked the value of the object to a pirate, a rather impetuous young man named Hoon, of improbable ancestry and unpredictable future. If we cannot have it, it's better that the other side does not, and so Hoon may help us while trying to help himself."

"But what if he beats Fer-de-lance to it?"

"Oh," smiled Peebles. "Then we'll steal it from Hoon."

"But that's likely to be difficult, isn't it?"

Peebles seized his opportunity. "That's why I have been ordered to tell you to gear up the entire operation. You, Viper, Asp, Cottonmouth, Copperhead, Water Moccasin—was he really an Olympic-class swimmer? get ready to shift everything to Southeast Asia. The, um, Fer-de-lance may need help, and you're to give it. If it's too late to help him, you're to either work with, or steal the object from, Hoon the pirate."

The Cobra was electrified. "*All* of us? Go out there? At one time? Steal?"

"Uh-huh."

"It's *dangerous,*" shouted Cobra. "And probably *dirty!*"

"Nevertheless," said Peebles, mildly, "those are your orders."

"*Damn!*"

Peebles coughed again. "There are compensations."

"Such as?"

"I hear the Asian girls are wonderful, if you know what I mean."

"Oh, *God!*"

There was a silence that finally made Peebles nervous and he coughed again. "There's more," he said.

"I can hardly wait," said Cobra, coldly.

"I mean we have to talk about your cover and your papers and so forth."

"Why don't you just tell it to Black Snake, he's our logistics officer. And yes, he's black." Cobra was beginning to find Peebles tiresome.

"All right," Peebles said, and got up to leave.

"What cover?" asked Cobra.

"What?"

"I said, what cover?"

Peebles shuffled. "Well, we ran you all through the computer and tried to find a common denominator, so you could all behave logically . . . you know, find something you all have in common."

"Well?"

"The only thing we could find is that at one time or another all of you studied music briefly . . . all of you play an instrument of one kind or another, and so . . ."

"No," said Cobra, aghast. "No."

". . . musical ambassadors of good will, playing American folk music . . ."

"No!"

"A folk music band on tour for the State Department. Perfect cover . . ."

"No, no, no, no, no, no, no, no, no, no!"

The door closed softly.

MOSCOW

The Chief of Four Section, KGB, sat in a small and unheated room which had only one window, high and narrow and barred. In the winter the Chief had to sit at his desk in his greatcoat; in the summer he peeled down to his underwear. There was little furniture in the room; his desk had two hard, utilitarian chairs in front of it, side by side and facing him. On one wall hung a portrait, and he had to refer to it from time to time because it was the head of his division, and the picture changed often. Each time he put up a new picture he thought about his own future. In lesser offices throughout the building his own photo was hanging, and he wondered when it, too, would be changed. He had noticed that all official portraits from the Workers' Portrait Bureau came in hinged glass frames, for easy replacement.

On another wall hung a set of chains ending in wrist irons. Sometimes, when he had to work late at the office it was necessary to bring a prisoner up here for conference, hence the chains. The Chief sighed; he had spent much of his life in similar offices, and he felt lucky to be still occupying space of any kind. So many of his contemporaries had shown imperialistic/capitalistic/counterproductive tendencies that they were no longer a part of the system. Any system. Lately he had thought more and more about them, but also lately he was finding it harder and harder to remember their names. He thought a lot about the French girl he had met once when he was escorting a scientist in the West. Ah, the West. Ah, the French girl . . .

He shook himself. Decadent thoughts. They interrupted his work.

He bent back over the single sheet of gray-white paper and he wrote with the stub of a pencil he had stolen from a hotel in Belgrade. He was readying a message for Petrov, and he could see Boris in his mind as he wrote the message.

SENDER: Four Section, KGB. For: Bangkok Station, relay to Petrov. D/T Grp 4061300. All follows for Petrov only. Acknowledge and comply.

Comrade! We salute you.

Reference by D/T Grp 6061215. It has been decided here by the head of my Division, Comrade M_____, that you probably require some assistance in complying with my above-referenced message. Not that we do not trust you, you understand, but that the importance of this mission is critical to advancements here—his, mine, and yours. The rabble-rousing assassins of the American Intelligence forces have created a situation in your sector which may impair our continued efforts to bring peace and stability to that part of the world.

Therefore, Comrade, we are taking the liberty of sending to you reinforcements. They will come under guise, of course, because we do not want to provoke the impetuous Americans into blundering into a costly mistake which could trigger another Great War. As you probably do not know, we employ a Manchurian acrobatic team whose loyalty to Mother Russia is unquestioned. They are adept at breaking and entering above the first floor. One of them holds the world's record for hanging by his teeth from a hovering helicopter on three kilometers of dental floss. They are all good boys, if a trifle hard to understand because of their dialect. But you must trust them and use them. I will send them to Bangkok Station, where they will be told to get all the publicity possible in the local Press, so that you will be able to contact them and use them in any way. They are accomplished assassins, codebreakers, chess players, and knife throwers.

Also reference my D/T 6061215, make it five yards instead of four of the dark red heavyweight Thai silk. Anya is several sizes larger than you might remember her, I'm afraid. When she is bored, she eats. I do not understand why she is bored. I tell her about my work . . . we go to political seminars together . . . I bring her the newest Russian Army Field Manuals. But you know how women are, never satisfied, eh, Comrade?

The Chief put the pencil down. Maybe he was telling too much, but there were so few people left to talk to, these days. He began again.

Do not let our people on Station get too involved in this project. They are indigenous personnel, and therefore not to be trusted with truly important matters concerning their country. Objectivity goes out the window, Comrade, when subjectivity comes in the door. Old Ukrainian saying. In other words, order the acrobats to leap a chasm for you and they will do it. Do not involve any of the local people because they are not to be confused with choices. When the mission is finished, send the acrobats home and report to head of Station, Paris *if* your mission has been successful. If it has *not*, and I hesitate to inject this negative note, Comrade, you will report here to me at once. At once, da?

But let us think on a positive note. Having retrieved the stolen object and its contents, you will quickly realize its importance and you will react promptly and properly. Use the diplomatic courier, as I previously instructed you. A few more photographs would be nice . . . Maybe you could find a different girl this time?

He closed the message imploring Petrov to continue his daily self-examination and confession period—"better than meditation"—and exhorted him to do his best. He signed it. Then the Chief locked his office and took the single sheet of paper down to the message center for relay to Petrov. A few minutes later he was out in the courtyard, watching the acrobats at practice.

There were five of them, lean and tough. They reminded him of Manchurian ponies, wiry and ageless, but they moved on steel-spring legs and their timing was unerring. They were superb physical specimens, and he thoughtfully patted his growing girth and thought vaguely of cutting out starch. But what was left?

He turned for the entrance. Maybe tonight he could draw Anya into the discussion of Napoleon's Russian campaign and the logistics breakdowns. She had been close to it the night before, but he could hear her snoring as he began to develop his theories. Ah, well. Who could understand a woman?

THE JUNGLE

The Old One was urinating off the back side of the sanctuary when he heard footsteps on the other side. Unperturbed, he glanced over his shoulder and saw his brother. He was very pleased. Hitching his pants up he turned and greeted him, gesturing him to a seat on the floor of the sanctuary. "The early bird gets the worm," said the Old One, absently.

"Never mind," said his brother, embracing the Old One before taking his seat on the floor. "You don't have to play the guru with me, you old pickpocket."

The Old One was startled. "Play? Play?"

"I'm only teasing," said his brother, whose name was Panam. "I've just come for a visit, Old One. I am on a job."

"What job?"

"I am taking around a very strange little man who says he is a zoologist named James Bonde. We have been on both sides of the river, here and in Laos. Sometimes I wonder if he knows what he is looking for. He seems very nervous."

"Ah."

"He is American."

"Ah. Not a sailor?"

"That young fool, Thanat, sent him with me to look for rare birds and animals. But he does not seem to be interested in the things that I have shown him. He keeps asking questions about the different villages and the village headmen, and if the villages receive a lot of visitors from the south. Also, he is very upset about his own bird, a creature named Phineas. It seems he and Phineas were very close, but at the first sight of a beautiful jungle bird, Phineas flew away. He disappeared in a flash of color and a raucous cry. Bonde seemed to think he was disloyal, and mourned the loss of what he called his drinking buddy. Westerners are strange, are they not?"

"But what is he looking for?"

"No idea," Panam grunted. "But he is determined, and as I said, very nervous. He is afraid of the shoreline when we are in the boat, and afraid of the passing boats when we are on shore."

The Old One looked up, suddenly. "Boats?" Panam nodded.

The Old One clambered to his feet and roared "Boats?"

Panam was startled. "What is it?"

"The boat" said the Old One. "They will come for it, of course."

"Have you been alone too long, my brother?"

The Old One paused and waited until he was calmer. When he spoke again his voice was a whisper. "He is the first. Others will come. I know they will. I think I have always known they would, but it has not been a bother until now that they are here."

Panam looked about, impatiently. "What are you *talking* about?"

"Sit down," said the Old One, his eyes on some distant place.

"I am sitting down. *You* sit down. What's the matter with you?"

"I know what your zoologist is looking for."

"*You* know?" The Old One nodded, the wise and calm look back in his eyes.

Panam felt his skin crawl. Maybe his older brother *did* have some kind of power. Panam had, for years, regarded him as a fraud. But now he seemed to know something. When Panam spoke again there was a new note of respect in his voice. "Is it something you can tell me, my brother?"

The Old One looked up. "Where is the zoologist now?"

"At the docks by the river. We are having the boat fixed; it has been leaking much lately, and so has he, as a matter of fact. I do not believe the Americans can absorb our food and water. He has spent a lot of time squatting and groaning. But he has not stopped searching."

"Yes," said the Old One, "they will not give up. The greed of the world is limitless; the perfidy of nations is unbounded; the avarice of man is unceasing; the—"

"Yes, yes," interrupted Panam. "But what is it they are looking for?"

The Old One looked at his brother a long time, then made up his mind. "I will tell you," he said. "Then you must bring the zoologist here. And I must trust you, Panam, because there is much greed connected with what I am about to say."

"You can trust me," Panam said, his curiosity rising.

"You have been to the Wat Arun and to the Temple of the Emerald Buddha, and the Temple of the Reclining Buddha, and . . ."

"Yes, yes," said Panam. "All in Bangkok. I have seen them all.

"And you have seen the great art treasures, and the statuary and the vases, and . . ."

"Yes, yes."

"Part of our story takes place in Bangkok. Part of it I do not know. But the real beginning . . ." the Old One paused. "Are you sure I can trust you?"

Panam was beside himself. *"Yes!"* he shouted.

"Then calm yourself," the Old One said soothingly. "No need to get upset."

"I'm sorry, my brother," said Panam, beginning to sweat. The Old One settled back on his haunches and prepared to tell his story in an orderly fashion, one thing at a time.

Panam, transfixed, watched his brother's eyes as the Old One began his story.

"It starts in Mongolia more than seven hundred years ago, in the *ordu*—the tent—of a man called Temujin, known to the world as the Scourge of God, the Perfect Warrior, the Mighty Manslayer, the Master of Thrones and Crowns. He was Genghis Khan . . ."

"Would you consider untying me now?" Natalya asked sweetly. She was sitting in the shade of a large-leafed tree, legs tucked under her demurely. Stratton was lying on the other side of the tree with sweat staining every inch of his clothing, but his hair was combed and the neatly graying temple showed even whiter in the midday shade.

MacTavish sat facing Natalya, looking and feeling like the wrath of God. His mouth was dry, he was sweating, and the jungle insects had set up a continual buzzing in his ears that had become a torrent of noise.

"Come on, Mac," said Natalya, "I won't call you Clarendon anymore."

"You won't run away?"

"Where would I go?"

"To find Boris?"

"What for?"

"You're spying for him, aren't you?"

"Do you think that's the only reason I am here?"

"For God's sake," rumbled Stratton. "Do you have to talk in questions?"

MacTavish squinted at her. "Why else would you be here?"

"Do you really want to know?"

Stratton sat up. "We all want to know. The whole world wants to know. Try to do it in sentences."

"I talk better untied."

MacTavish walked over and cut her loose with the small pocket knife he carried. He sat closer to her in the shade. "We're listening."

"It's short and simple. I do it for the adventure of it. I cannot resist the kind of excitement that comes from doing something new and different. It's almost"—she lowered her eyes—"sexual."

"Sex can be an adventure," said MacTavish, suddenly wondering how he could get rid of Stratton for a while.

"My God, yes," said Stratton, wondering if he could lose MacTavish for a bit. Anyone could see this young lady was taken with him.

"Has it always been this way for you?" MacTavish asked.

"Since I was a little girl in Moscow. I wanted to go everywhere, do everything. We were not rich, but not poor, you understand? I was good in languages and the Party sent me to the Worker's Paradise Translation and Interpreters' Commune. It was opening the door on a very exciting future. I have been many places now, and had good adventures." She flashed a perfect smile at MacTavish and Stratton, who watched her with growing lust. "I believe," she said, "life is meant to be enjoyed. Or else what's it for?"

"My God, yes," Stratton said for the second time.

"So you're not one of the ideologically pure?" MacTavish asked.

She looked at him steadily. "Not really."

"It's the excitement, then," MacTavish said.

"Yes."

"Then tell us what this is all about," MacTavish said gently. "It's not very exciting to bang around in the jungle waiting for old Boris to come back and shoot us, which he will surely do. Let's find out what this to-do is all for, and maybe we can get out of this mess."

Natalya hesitated. "Now you will think I am holding out on you. The truth is, I don't know very much. We were assigned to get you here from Hong Kong so you could help us find our way around upcountry, to make sure we didn't miss any villages of any size. There aren't very good maps of this area."

"I know," said MacTavish.

"Boris wouldn't tell me much else. We are looking for

something that was stolen in Bangkok and carried north to one of these villages. It's an *objet d'art,* but something more. There's something inside it which everyone wants, including the Americans. They have activated an Intelligence unit which has been dormant for eighteen years and—"

"Eighteen years?" said MacTavish, astonished.

"Isn't that a long time?" asked Stratton.

"Eighteen years," Natalya said. "There was a double agent inside the unit, and he told my superiors about the mission. The Americans are here to try to recover it as well. I wish I knew what's inside it, but Boris wouldn't tell me. I don't think he knows himself. Anyway, the difficulty is, we have to go to various villages, and these people are supposed to be very, uh—"

"Asian," said Stratton.

"Closed-mouth. Taciturn," said MacTavish.

"Yes. Well. But we have to find it before Boris finds you," Natalya said. "Or before he finds *us,* I guess. He probably thinks I'm a traitor."

MacTavish pondered. "The thing to do," he said slowly, "is to get to either the village headman or the gurus. Usually they're the ones who know what's happening." He stood up.

"Over there," he pointed, "is the Mekong. The villages lie along it and use it as a highway to the markets. You also have to cross it to get to Laos. If I'd stolen something in Thailand and had gotten this far, I'd head for the Laos border, just to get out of the country. So . . . let's head for Laos, hitting the villages nearest us. You don't know the jungle telegraph like I do. We ask in one village about something stolen in Bangkok and they'll be hiding things in villages a hundred miles away before dark."

"All right," Stratton said, standing and brushing himself off. "Let's get going." It was time, he thought, to take command of the situation. He was trying to be very attentive and observant. The Joint Chiefs of Staff might be interested in this. And his public would want to know about his adventures in the jungle in very fine detail. It would be worth a whole series. He'd have to get it on the air before that damned ink-washed savage, MacTavish, could get it into print. MacTavish probably would distort it to make himself the hero. If he, Stratton, hadn't stood up in the jeep to get the Russian's attention, MacTavish might never have been able to get away.

They started walking east, MacTavish leading. Once Stratton took the lead without asking, and MacTavish let him break trail for a while before Stratton began to wander off course; then MacTavish, followed by Natalya, simply flowed around him. After that, Stratton stayed in the rear.

The bush they walked through now was beginning to thin, and once they came upon a small farm, giving the farm dogs hysteria. They skirted it and came back on course and kept moving eastward throughout the long morning. By noon they were resting again. MacTavish was parched and knew they would have to find either a bottle of scotch or a drink of water soon. As they got up to leave, he heard Natalya's stomach rumble charmingly. She was hungry, but not complaining.

Late in the afternoon they caught sight of the Mekong. It was quite a way off, but it was the magnet for the northeast, as it was much of the Southeast Asia peninsula. The great river began in China and emptied in the South China Sea, a tremendous life-giving force to millions. The three of them stood on a little knoll and stared at it.

"It's a bit far," said Natalya.

MacTavish agreed. "We can't do it in one day without telling the world we're here. We'll go until dark, sleep one more night, then try to hit a village tomorrow. At least we can get food and water."

"Why are we being so sneaky, MacTavish?" Stratton wanted to know. "Are you afraid of something?"

MacTavish eyes him. "You're either dumb or foolish, Stratton—"

"Don't forget, your stupidity is the only reason I'm here," Stratton cut in, hotly.

"Well, we don't want old Boris to know about us until we know where *he* is, do we?"

"Have it your way," Stratton said. "For now." For Stratton, the problem was not that difficult. They could simply find a village, he would tell them who he was, and half the foreign ministers of the world would send aircraft to pick him up. What was so complicated about that? He was a resource that MacTavish, in his ignorance, chose not to use.

They walked through the long afternoon, watching the shadows stretch and feeling the welcome coolness of the evening. Just before dusk they found a small clearing, still in hilly, slightly rolling country. MacTavish hoped the snakes were somewhere else. "This'll do," he said.

The three of them went different ways in the bush just before dark fell. MacTavish decided not to risk a fire and the three of them lay down, Natalya in the center for warmth, for the night. MacTavish was very conscious of her smell, mixed with sweat, and the touch of her body along his. Stratton pretended to touch her by accident and she gave him an amused look which was more devastating than a slap might have been.

Exhausted, MacTavish gave himself a few minutes to fantasize about her, and began dropping off into a deep sleep. When he awoke it was just after dawn, still gray and not yet hot. He turned to look at Natalya. She was sleeping with her mouth slightly open, showing perfect teeth.

And Stratton was gone.

". . . and so I got rid of it," the Old One concluded.

Panam sat, spellbound. Finally he spoke. "That's one *hell* of a story!"

"Yes, isn't it," agreed the Old One. The two brothers sat in silence for a time.

"Well," said Panam. "I'm not going to ask you where you put it."

"You see," said the Old One. "Even you are hinting for it. Even you are touched by it."

"Untrue," said Panam. "I am curious as to how the story finally will end."

"Yang and yin," said the Old One.

"What?"

"Calm before the storm."

"What?"

"The question is," said the Old One, "whether we tell your zoologist, James Bonde, what we have here and find out what he intends to do about it."

"A very good question," Panam agreed.

"But it is not proper for a guru to be involved in such matters," said the Old One suddenly. "I am no longer a professional man."

"I will handle it for you," said Panam eagerly.

"For a percentage, like some literary agent?" asked the Old One.

Panam put his hand to his heart. "You pain me, my brother. I will simply try to help the village out of this situation. You see, if everyone comes looking for it, the life of the village will be upset, maybe forever."

The Old One thought. "Maybe you're right," he said.

"Then tell me where it is," Panam said triumphantly, "and I will dispose of it before the others arrive, and the village will be safe and undisturbed."

"You seem eager," said the Old One, suspiciously.

"Trust me," said Panam gently.

"Cross you heart and hope to die," said the Old One. "I am doing this only for the sake of the village."

When Panam did not answer, the Old One looked up at him. Panam was staring down the trail, an expression of anguish on his face. "It's too late," he cried.

"What is it?" asked the Old One.

"Look!" The Old One stood and peered.

Up the trail came a band of men, led by a tall young man

with a long mustache and carrying an evil-looking gun. Behind him, walking single file, the tough-looking men also were heavily armed. And in front of him, the leader was pushing a small American with thick glasses and a funny hat. They were heading straight for the sanctuary.

"Everything in moderation," mumbled the Old One.

Panam looked at him. "What does it mean?"

"Bandits," said the Old One. "Pirates."

The men had seen them now and the tall young one broke into a huge grin and began to shout.

"Guru! Old One! At last we have found you!"

The Old One looked at him curiously, watching them approach. He was a strong young man, probably ruthless, mused the Old One. The man in front—this must be the zoologist Bonde—was less impressive, but he must have put up some kind of a fight, because his hands were tied behind him and there was a dark bruise on his cheek.

As the Old One watched, the men reached the sanctuary, and like well-trained troops, fanned around it with outposts watching in four directions. The leader and his prisoner stopped directly in front of the Old One and Panam, who stood staring down at them. "Hello, Old One," said the young man pleasantly. "I am Hoon, the pirate." The Old One nodded.

"I am Panam," said Panam to Hoon. "Brother to the Old One."

"And these are my men," Hoon gestured.

"And this must be Bonde," said the Old One.

"Are the introductions over?" asked Farley, grumpily.

Hoon laughed. "Do you have to catch a train to somewhere?"

The Old One sighed. What to do now?

"Listen, Guru, Old One," said Hoon earnestly. "You know of something we seek, I think. We have heard of it, even in Macau. Bonde here is looking for it. I think others may be, from the way Bonde talks. Tell us where it is?"

"The wind cannot read," said the Old One. Hoon stared at him.

"Riches cannot buy happiness, young pirate," said the Old One.

"But it will buy everything else," said Hoon, "and then I will have everything, for I am already happy."

"If you are happy, why do you seek more?" Panam asked, resentful of the pirates and worried about what they might do.

"Because the seeking is what makes me happy," Hoon explained, smiling.

"You're a damned pirate, you bastard," Farley hissed.

"And you," replied Hoon, "are a lucky man, for you have led me to the Old One. Without seeing you squatting in the bushes near the dock we might never have stopped here. And so, when this is over, we will let you go."

"This isn't over yet!"

"True," said Hoon, turning to business. "Old One, will you tell us where you hid it . . . and exactly what it is?" But before the Old One could answer, one of Hoon's lookouts whistled like a jungle bird. Everyone froze.

Hoon gestured and the pirates dropped into a crouch. The Old One and Panam stood very still, watching Hoon. The young pirate was intent on a clump of trees down the hill on the other side of the sanctuary. "Don't fire," Hoon said quietly. For long moments they watched, then they heard the slight noise again, someone pushing through the bushes. They saw the bushes part.

A man staggered out, disheveled and sweating. His clothes were torn and he was panting. There was a wild look in his eye. All of the guns of Hoon's men were trained on him. He saw them at once and stared at the guns. "Don't shoot," he said hoarsely. "Don't shoot. My producer would never forgive you."

"Who the hell are *you?*" inquired Hoon.

The man drew himself up and threw back his head to stare

at Hoon, incredulous and upset. "You mean you don't know?"

"My God," Farley said suddenly, "it's Sidney Stratton, the television reporter!"

"And commentator," Stratton added.

There was a short silence, broken abruptly by Hoon. "A newsman, eh? I can guess why you're here. You're looking for it, too."

"I am looking for a way the hell out of here," Stratton said testily.

"Then you come with us and when this is all over we'll turn you loose, along with James Bonde here. I like to travel light."

Fer-de-lance looked at Stratton, some of his bravado returning. "Play ball with them," he said to Stratton. "I'll get us out of this."

"But the key to all of this lies with the Old One," Hoon said. "And so we must now ask him politely if he will help us. Old One?"

The Old One looked down at the circle of men. *It is time to reestablish some control here; I am the guru, after all, and this is my village.* "First there is something I must do," the Old One said. He padded over to one corner of the sanctuary where a dirty cotton blanket was wrapped around a well-worn mat. He sat and stretched and swung his legs up onto the mat, turning on his left side. To their astonishment, the Old One began to snore.

One of Hoon's men swore and started forward but Hoon waved him back, grinning hugely. "It is the sleep of the innocent," Hoon said. "We will wait for him to awake. Meanwhile, let us be comfortable. Is anyone hungry? I am. Piracy is hard work." And he sat on the steps of the sanctuary while two of the pirates ran back down the trail to the village in search of food. Stratton and Farley sat in the shade of a tree, whispering to each other. Panam, too nervous to rest, sat alone with his thoughts. The sun climbed higher and the heat washed over all of them as they listened to the Old One's snores.

"But why is it so important to find him?" Natalya asked.

They were hurrying along in the wake of bent tree limbs and broken bushes left by Stratton's precipitous crashing through the jungle. MacTavish, thirsty, hungry, tired, and now angry, barked his answer.

"Because he's such a simple shit. Several things could happen. One, and likely, is that he'll wander in a circle and come back here eventually if he doesn't run into Boris first, and lead Boris back here. Two, he'll run into somebody else and tell his story and they'll think he's crazy, and we'll get no help. Three, he'll break a leg, and much as I'm pissed at him at the moment, we can't leave him up here to die. And four, and not the least of my worries, is that he'll go off and get this on the air—half-assed as usual—and while I don't mind using him if I have to, I sure as hell want to beat him on the story.

"If," he added, "I ever find out exactly what the story is."

After a while they stopped to rest. "We're making better time than Stratton," MacTavish said. "He was ploughing around in the dark most of the time. I think we can catch him." He looked at Natalya, enjoying the way her breasts curved against the shirt-front. Her skin was glowing and her eyes shone, and her hair hung natural and beautiful over her shoulders. MacTavish suddenly felt one hundred and ten years old. "Stratton or no, I'm going to lie down for a few minutes."

He stretched out and looked up at the umbrella trees. When he had been up here once before he had lain under the trees like this with a young Thai girl, whose name he couldn't pronounce but whose tenderness and creativity were a delight to recall. They had met in the Air India ticket office in Bangkok, and she had said her father was from Calcutta and her mother a Thai. She was statuesque and gifted with a rare sense of humor, and they had had a magnificent two weeks in a little river sawmill town north of Korat, where the villagers came down to the river and bathed alongside the elephants, the elephants tame and playful after a day of dragging logs out of the teak forest. In the mornings the sun came up quick and hot, and they had stirred and taken tea and small rice biscuits from the wife of the sawmill owner. He wrote through the heat of the day, putting the previous month's experiences on paper, the softness of the present a poignant contrast with the killings he had seen just days earlier across the border in Laos. He wrote of the opium wars and the religious wars and the ideological wars, and now and then he tried to write about the simple goodness of the up-country villagers and the logic with which they played out their lives in tune with the crops, the flow of the river, the lives and deaths of the elephants. It had been the best time, and the best writing. In the late afternoon she would bring him the first drink of the day—as every writer knew, the best one—and still later would take him down to the river and bathe him, unashamed, in front of all the other villagers, who laughed and waved and enjoyed having him around. When dark fell, they would light the single candle in the small room and make love very slowly and with great ease, caring for each other.

"Mac?" Natalya shook him awake.

He sat up and blinked at her. "I was dreaming. About being up here before."

"Must have been a girl in it; you were smiling."

MacTavish grunted.

"Was she pretty?"

"Why do women always ask that first?"

"To find out what the man is like. Your answer is very important, you see."

"We had a great time together . . . probably because it was temporary."

"And why was it?"

"I had to be on Quemoy shortly. After that I would go down to Mindanao and do a story on the cigarette smuggling. Sooner or later I would be back on the Plain of Jars in Laos, or back in Vietnam."

"I see."

"Was that the right answer?"

"Not for most men, Mac. But for you . . . it probably was the right answer."

"Why do I have a feeling I've been put down?"

She reached over and touched him, letting her hand rest lightly on his wrist. "You are faithful in your way, Mac, but never to a woman. I do not 'put you down,' but you are not meant for a happy marriage and a house full of children."

"My God, no! Who said I was?"

Natalya laughed. "Shouldn't we go?"

Stratton's trail remained easy to follow. Once in a while they would find a piece of torn clothing ("He'll be naked by the time we find him," MacTavish grinned), and often they could stand and see where he had woven a path through the jungle, kicking over small plants and breaking bush limbs.

In the midafternoon they came to a small rise, and caught a glimpse of village roofs. Above the humming of insects they thought they could hear the flowing of the Mekong as it channeled into gorges and spread out again in a giant watery fan. Stratton's trail led straight toward the village and they knew he must have seen the rooflines as well.

"We'd better catch up before he gets us into more trouble," MacTavish said, beginning to jog down the rise. Natalya followed, smiling. It was MacTavish who had gotten Stratton in trouble, but men were such children she didn't bother to remind him. They had moved downward not more than a hundred yards when they burst into a clearing and stopped, thunderstruck.

Stratton sat under a tree with another Caucasian, a funny-looking little man in thick glasses and an old-fashioned pith helmet. In the center of the clearing was a small, typical up-country shrine-sanctuary with two men on it, staring at them. On the steps was a tall young man carrying a very modern rifle. And all around them was a wicked-looking group of men with knives and guns, and the guns were leveled at them.

The tall young man stood and leaned his gun against the steps and put his hands on his hips. He spoke excellent English: "I feel like this is Queen's Road Central, in downtown Hong Kong. Are there any more out there?"

Stratton leaped to his feet. "You followed me!"

Farley unfolded and rose also. His bonds had been cut. "Who are you? What's this all about?"

The Old One peered at them. "It is a wise man who knows what *anything* is all about." Panam threw up his hands in despair. "Is the whole world coming here?" he asked, of no one in particular.

MacTavish shook his head. "By Jesus Christ, by Joe Namath, by Ernest Hemingway . . ." He swung around to Natalya.

She was standing very erect, very watchful, and there was a strange glint in her eye. She was watching Hoon. She saw first the fine body, then the mustache which framed his chin in parentheses, and his fine features. "He has eyes like a hawk," she whispered.

"Huh?" said MacTavish.

"He is magnificent," she whispered again. And now Hoon had seen her. He saw first the fine body, then the hair which framed her face, and her fine features. He saw the steppes of Central Asia in her tilting eyes and he saw more: the finely honed sense of adventure, the total absence of fear.

"What are you called?" he said gently, and began to walk toward her.

"I am Natalya Vorshova."

"Russian?" She nodded.

He stopped in front of her, his eyes never leaving hers. "I am a pirate," he said. "My name is Hoon."

"Hoon? Chinese?"

"A little. And a little Portuguese and a little Scot. And maybe a little Aleut, for all I know. Does it matter?"

"Oh, no," Natalya breathed. She felt her breast moving a bit rapidly, something Hoon did not fail to notice.

"What are you doing here?" he asked her.

"Excuse me," said MacTavish, with heavy sarcasm. "I do so hate to break up a social affair, but do you think the troops could put away their instruments before one goes off, and could we sit in the shade? If it isn't too much goddamned trouble."

For a long moment he was ignored. Hoon and Natalya were searching each other's faces and MacTavish watched with interest. It was the first time Natalya was not in control of the man; if anything, she was breathing faster and there were two faint spots of color in her cheeks. She had crossed her arms and was standing, shy as any schoolgirl, in Hoon's penetrating gaze. *She's done for,* MacTavish thought. *Done for, by a damned pirate. I might have known.*

"We were looking for Sidney Stratton. Over there," she answered finally, pointing at Stratton.

"And what is *he* doing here, that you search for him?"

Natalya brushed her hair back in a very feminine gesture. Hoon was charmed. "It's a rather long story," she said.

"I have time," Hoon said gently. "Shall we get out of the sun?" And he turned and led her up the steps of the sanctuary, MacTavish following and feeling foolish. Behind him, then, came Stratton and Farley, muttering to each other. Hoon's men continued to surround the sanctuary.

When they were arranged around the small sanctuary, sitting on the floor and waiting expectantly, Hoon uncorked a bottle of fine scotch. MacTavish sat up and felt his nose twitch. Provisions at last! Hoon passed around the bottle and MacTavish took a long pull, feeling his limbs tingle and the life start to flow back into him. *Now, now we'll see about this little matter.*

Then Hoon passed around some food from the village. It

was rice, cooked with coconut milk in a shaft of bamboo, and some pieces of broiled pork with onion. Natalya ate ravenously, but kept her eyes on Hoon. Farley paled at the sight of food and Stratton ate only the rice. As they ate, Hoon and MacTavish began a rotation of the scotch between them. After a time, Hoon stood and said, "All right. What's going on here?"

They all began to talk at once and Hoon threw up his hands. "One at a time," he said, and pointed to MacTavish. "You first."

MacTavish told him all he knew, and Hoon then pointed to Natalya. She told him everything, including the fact that the Americans were sending secret agents to intercept them with the stolen object. Hoon pointed to Stratton, who protested he had been kidnapped and was merely trying to get to his cameraman and on the air. Farley claimed he was the zoologist, Dr. James Bonde, and felt immediately that nobody believed him.

At the end they all had the same information, except for one thing, and at last Hoon turned to the Old One. "Now," he said softly, but with a hint of steel in his voice, "it is your turn, Old One. What is it that we all seek? And where is it?"

The Old One sighed. It was time.

"Once upon a time," he began, and the group leaned forward expectantly. The Old One stopped and glanced at their faces. "All good stories begin with once upon a time," he explained. MacTavish took another pull of the scotch, feeling stronger by the minute, and settled back to listen.

"Once upon a time," the Old One continued, "and this is a story every educated person in our country knows . . .

"The great Genghis Khan was sitting in his tent, surrounded by some of the people he liked best. There was Soo, the great crossbowman; there was the crafty general, Muhuli, who bore many battle scars; there was the other general, Bayan, with his wide network of spies; there were the Khan's first brothers-in-arms, Borchu and Kassar. And there was Arghun.

"Arghun was the one they turned to for a song or a story. He was the gentle spirit among the great Khan's inner court. But this day Arghun was in deep trouble. Temujin—Genghis Khan—had asked him to play a song on the Khan's favorite golden lute. Alas, Arghun had borrowed it, but lost it.

"Enraged, the Khan ordered Arghun's death. Two paladins took Arghun out as if to kill him, but the fun-loving Mongols made him drink two huge skins of wine, to keep his life. Arghun drank and drank, and passed out." The Old One looked at MacTavish, who was tilting the bottle of scotch, and lifted his eyebrows. "Moderation in all things," the guru said.

MacTavish nodded agreeably.

"The next day the paladins roused Arghun and took him in to see the Khan. Seizing the moment, Arghun burst into song, a song about how he loved to drink, but was no thief. Genghis Khan pardoned him on the spot."

The Old One stopped again and looked around the circle. He had them in the palms of his hands.

"But what happened to the golden lute? To historians, it remains a mystery. But legend has it that the lute was stolen from Arghun's tent by a low, cunning thief. Soon after, the thief was caught stealing something else, and was tied to four horses who then galloped with pieces of him across the steppes in four different directions. The lute was taken by a friend of the dead thief, who was so afraid of it that he kept it hidden until he, too, died.

"By now it was dangerous to have the lute; instead of something valuable it had become something dangerous to possess. Finally, at some point, someone burned the wooden parts but kept the gold, molded into a simple gold bar.

"But the gold bar is said now to possess demons. It was in a ship when the Mongol invaders sailed to conquer Japan, and a typhoon sank many ships.

"Then it was reported in the possession of a king of Burma in 1283, when Burma fell to the Mongols. The gold bar was in a Mongol invading force ten years later, when the force was attacked by natives and wiped out. It ended up in Shang-tu, which is also called Xanadu. There it stayed for a time. It became known as Xanadu Gold.

"Then the scene shifts. A Yuan general had the gold bar melted down again and made into a sword handle.

"Meanwhile, the court at Shang-tu had become a mixture of Arabs, Mohammedans, Venetians. Foreign ideas were introduced. And as usual, there followed a Chinese revival. A Ming emperor took over in Nanking, and a Ming army entered Shang-tu. In time, the Ming emperor Yung-lo was receiving tribute from Korea, the Ryukyus, Annam, Champa, Cambodia, Siam, Borneo—even lavish tribute from the Japanese. It was a very turbulent time in China. And as you know when the wolves are walking, the rabbits feel the earth tremble.

"The general's sword handle by now was a breastpiece, and then it became the decorative covering for a scabbard. In time it became what it is today."

Hoon leaned forward expectantly. "And that is . . ."

The Old One held up his right hand. "Do not be impatient."

Natalya glanced at Hoon, who felt her gaze on him. He turned to look at her, and MacTavish felt something pass between them. She nodded slightly, and Hoon sat back and waited.

"In the reign of Yung-lo there were great fleets of ships which sailed from China into Southeast Asia. They were under the command of the eunuch, Cheng Ho, who was a Moslem. He first sailed to India with sixty-two ships and nearly thirty thousand men. There were other voyages, and when they had ended, Yung-lo was dead and the gold bar had been melted down once again and made into a small golden ship. A Chinese trading junk. And that's what it is today."

There was a stunned silence.

"And that's it?" MacTavish nearly yelled. Hoon was on his

feet. "I can buy a room full of those," he stormed. "That is not a fantastic treasure!"

"There's more," chuckled the Old One, enjoying his moment.

"Then get on with it," Hoon snapped, his patience thinning.

"It seems," continued the Old One, "that each time the gold changed owners, or was changed, the new owners, for some reason, for luck perhaps, kept the mysterious inscription inside of it. At first it appeared to be crude calligraphy, but then it was interpreted as a map. That's what it looked like to me."

"To you!" Farley was on his feet, his cheeks flushed. "You've seen it?"

"Hell," said MacTavish. "He's not only seen it. He's got it. Haven't you?"

The Old One smiled.

"Listen," Farley's words came in a rush. "We'll buy it from you. Whatever you want for it. It's best if it is in the United States. My government sent me here to find it, and I am empowered to get it at whatever cost. So name your price."

"Shut up," Hoon ordered curtly, and turned back to the Old One. "So what makes the inscription valuable?"

"It is supposed to show," said the Old One slowly, "a section of the Great Wall of China.

MacTavish grinned at the Old One. "You keep leaving out bits and pieces of your story."

"I haven't made up my mind yet," said the Old One.

"Make it up, guru," said Hoon menacingly, but the Old One was not perturbed. He shifted and looked out of the sanctuary. It was getting toward evening now; there would be a quick dusk and nightfall, and it was time to get these strangers out of his sanctuary.

"In the days of the Mongols," the Old One resumed, "there was much tribute. One rampaging general amassed a fortune so large he became frightened of it. As always, immense riches ruled the man. Finally, after an act of treachery had opened the gates of a tower on the Great Wall, his men had time to hide the treasure in the Wall, then mortar it up again. I suppose it is there today, and the inscription in the junk shows where to find it."

They sat very still. Finally MacTavish asked, "Is there more?"

"No," said the Old One.

"Why hasn't anyone gone after the map before this?" asked MacTavish.

"It was in one of our temples," the Old One said. "It was a part of an offering to Buddha. As long as it was revered as such, and closely guarded, then it was untouchable. When it was stolen, it became a treasure—a ship to be salvaged, like any other. And sailors"—he turned and spat out of the sanctuary—"are used to taking what they want."

Stratton stirred. "Let me get this straight. What started out as a lute became a piece of gold and finally became a golden junk, but the real story is that inside it is a map showing where there's a treasure hidden in the Great Wall of China?"

"*Damn,* Sidney," MacTavish said, surprised, "that's a good wrap-up. I didn't know you could do it."

"Wait a minute," said Hoon. "That can't be all." They stared at the young pirate. "If it were just the treasure, then why are all the damned spies looking for it? What value does it have for a government?"

"Shit," said Farley, and they all turned to look at him. "I *knew* it would come to this." He stood again and pulled down his jacket and adjusted his glasses.

"My name is not James Bonde," he said dramatically. "I am Henderson Farley, an agent of the United States government, engaged in clandestine operations.

"We did not know all the guru knows about the history of the golden junk, but we knew about the map. We knew because the treasure was found a long time ago by accident by an American archaeologist trying to prove a relationship between Cathay and ancient Armenia. He is now in real estate in California, and the treasure has been confiscated by my government."

Hoon closed his eyes. He swore softly in Portuguese, with a few Cantonese obscenities for flavor. "But that doesn't answer the question," MacTavish said.

Farley looked embarrassed. "Do I have to?"

Hoon, still in a cold rage, lifted his gun and pointed it straight at Farley's narrow chest. "I see," Farley said.

"Go on, Mr. Farley," Natalya urged.

"After World War Two," Farley resumed in a whisper, "when there were lots of Americans in China, we anticipated we might go to war with the Communists. So we used the hidden place where the treasure had been to plant a nuclear explosive. After we planted the device we strung out several of them along the Great Wall. They are in place today, waiting to be blown. The Wall is about two thousand miles long; we could blow a great deal of it, anytime."

"But why should you?" asked Natalya, horrified.

"Oh, we wouldn't—now," Farley reassured her. "But your people are having some troubles with China, and your KGB wants to find the main device and the room in the Great Wall where it can be triggered. You see, the Soviets could blow it for their own reasons, or blow it after revealing to the world what we had done, and pretend it was an accident, or that we had done it. Either way, it would be bad for my government."

"To say nothing of the Chinese," said MacTavish bitingly. "They happen to have a great regard for their Wall."

"Well," said Farley, in an attempt at humor, "That's show biz."

Stratton looked at Farley with distaste. "You'd never make it in the electronic medium," he said. It was his strongest condemnation.

A silence fell over the group. MacTavish looked at the lengthening shadows outside the sanctuary and wished he were back in Wan Chai with Fu Manchu Two and Chow

Fun, drinking scotch in the How Far Inn and telling lies about girls. The thought prompted him to glance at Natalya, and just as he did, she asked the final question. "Where is the junk now, Old One?"

All eyes turned to the guru, who had been busy as Farley talked. He had been sitting closest to Stratton, so he had Stratton's eighteen-hundred-dollar Rolex under his mat, two .30 caliber shells from Hoon's shirt pocket which he had lifted for practice, and he had taken, examined, and replaced the contents of one of Hoon's pirate's wallet.

The Old One let the drama build for a moment.

"It's where a junk should be," he said. "On the river."

THE RIVER

Hoon's junk rode at anchor, bow upstream, in the center of the narrow brown waterway. There were lanterns on the bow and stern and a rare, mild breeze came downriver, cooling the occupants of the deck and keeping the junk trim and steady on the river's heart. Hoon was at ease back on the junk, and he leaned against the railing near the stern and gazed deeply at Natalya, who leaned beside him. The smell of food cooking on charcoal fires mingled with the slight breeze, and stirred appetites already stirred by the excitement of the Old One's story, and its aftermath.

Across from them MacTavish was deep in conversation with Stratton.

"Christ, Sidney," he was saying, "what kinda film you planning to use with a story like this? Aerial footage of the Southeast Asian peninsula? Pictures of life-size Chinese junks, saying it looks like this only smaller, and older, and made out of gold? No, Sidney, this one is for the print guys, and I'll have it out two hours after we're back in Bangkok."

"Well let *me* ask *you*," Stratton said huffily, "are you going to tell the world we planted atomic bombs in China after World War Two?"

"I certainly am," said MacTavish. "People have a right to know."

"It was done," said Farley, who had been eavesdropping, "by a couple of generals without the knowledge and approval of the American government. The guilty ones have been punished. Controls are much tighter now. The situation cannot happen again. Why not just let it go? You'll only stir up trouble."

"No, Farley. It's a hell of a story. And I'm going to tell every tiny bit of it. Maybe it'll keep you assholes on your toes in the future. How do I know—how do the American people know—we're not off plastering the Arc de Triomphe with *plastique?* Or hiding a little something in the Pyramids against the day we can say, 'surprise!' and trigger another war? *Huh?*"

"You'll have to take my word for it," Farley said, with dignity.

"Shit," said MacTavish. "That's what your word is worth."

Stratton yawned. He wished he were back in the Club, after a good bath and a bracing dinner. He would hold them spellbound with his account of these adventures. But first, he had to call his network. They probably would want him to brief the President.

". . . and so there you have it, Mr. President. We did all that was humanly possible, at some personal sacrifice . . ."

"Your nation is grateful, Mr. Stratton. It pleases me to be able to bestow these small awards as mere symbols of our esteem, and to congratulate you on your elevation to network news president . . ."

Panam sat near the bow, eating hungrily. He had returned to the dock with the others only to find his own boat sunk alongside the dock. His last glimpse of the Old One caused him to smile; his brother was waving an expensive gold watch and laughing. Panam had laughed in return, and faintly heard a parting admonition:

"There is nothing permanent," called the Old One, "except change." Panam had thought about that a lot in the past few hours. Crazy as it sounded, the Old One may have known what he talked about.

Natalya and Hoon, by accident or design, had worked their way farther aft on the junk. Hoon held the remnants of the bottle of scotch, and he passed it back and forth with Natalya, pleased to see she did not shrink from drinking out of the bottle. "And are you still shocked by the Old One's story?" he asked her.

"Just that nations do the things they do."

"And yet you are a part of doing such things."

"I *was* a part. It was an adventure for me. It's the sort of thing I like." She pushed back her hair. "I wish I had a place to take a bath."

Hoon smiled in the gathering darkness. "In my house in Macau there are many bathrooms. I offer you a bath in all of them."

"First we have to get there."

"We'll get there."

"But first we have to find the golden junk, and tell the Chinese government where the bombs are."

"If we can, we will. They will be very grateful, I hope. After all, I should get something out of this little trip."

"I thought you were happy just being up here," said Natalya, slightly resentful.

"I will be happier if I can take something back," Hoon said.

Natalya stood very still and looked at the shoreline. "It is better to give than receive, they say in the West."

"This is the Mekong River, and my usual home is the South China Sea. Does that apply there?"

"I think so," she said slowly. "And here."

Hoon reached out and gathered her in.

"I'm a mess," she said. "My hair is dirty; I need a bath. My skin is rough, my—"

"Shut up, woman," he said, and kissed her. She kissed him back. And again.

MacTavish saw their silhouette. He saw them turn and go

below to the aft compartment of the junk. He gave a long sigh. "Sidney, Farley, you are two of the most unlikely drinking mates a man ever had, but if we can find another bottle on this scow, I invite you to join me. In the bow."

"Do you suppose," Stratton asked as they moved forward, "they might have any rum and Coke?" And even Farley laughed.

During the night, MacTavish dreamed he was the navigator aboard the *Titanic,* and the ship was in trouble because he couldn't find the bridge to warn the captain about the icebergs. Later he dreamed that he was a Mongol general, and every time he rode near the Great Wall a bowman who looked like Hoon shot arrows at him. He awoke with the feeling he was inside a giant oven, being alternately baked and struck by an enormous wooden spoon wielded by the Old One, dressed as a chef. He was on deck and the sun was already up, and Hoon was standing over him.

"We need to hold a council of war," Hoon said gaily. He looked relaxed and confident. Beyond him, MacTavish could see Natalya, combing her hair with her fingers and looking radiant. *That's that.* Stratton and Farley sat against the forward cabin, looking old and ill, and MacTavish grinned at them. Stratton gave him one withering glance and buried his head in his hands. Farley acted stunned, and looked vacant.

But in a few minutes Hoon had them in a circle on deck. A crewman was preparing breakfast, reviving the charcoal from the night before, and cooking over five-gallon tins with air holes punched in the side. It took MacTavish immediately back to the rivers of Vietnam. Some things were universal . . .

"Pay attention, now," Hoon said, tugging on one side of his long mustache. "We must put our heads together." Natalya giggled, and Hoon looked at her happily. *Christ,* thought MacTavish. *It's high school days again.*

"Attention," I said. They all tried to look attentive.

"We cannot exactly fix the day or time, but the Old One said it was several days after the junk was brought to him. A young boy of the village came to the sanctuary with a small, flat boat, a toy he had made for use on the river. It is about two feet long and has a bamboo covering; that's where the Old One slipped the golden junk, just before he set it afloat. We know it was watertight, because the Old One saw it float away on the current. So all we have to do is search the riverbanks, both sides, and sooner or later we'll find it. Unless some curious villager or fisherman has picked it up by now."

"I don't understand why that old fool put it in the water anyway," Stratton grumbled.

"It was symbolic, Stratton," MacTavish said. "Here he had this object which had caused so much pain, and this little kid comes along with a toy boat, and he began to see a way of getting rid of it. He never thought we'd all descend on him like that. He was glad to be rid of it."

"He could just have thrown it away," Stratton argued.

"Sure, but this was somehow more fitting. Now we've got to try to get it back. How do you propose to do it, Hoon?"

"We'll put men ashore to run down the riverbanks. We don't want to interest the villagers. We will use this junk to search the fishing boats, in case it's been found. And I mean search—we take nobody's word for it. Meanwhile, we will borrow a few small boats and push in with them as close to the shoreline as we can get, to look under the overhang. We'll turn it up," he said confidently. "What's to stop us?"

Natalya gasped and sat upright. "Boris!" she shouted.

"What?" said Hoon.

MacTavish got to his feet. "Son of a bitch, I forgot all about him."

"What is a Boris?" Hoon asked.

"It is," MacTavish replied, "a large, evil man with a huge gun and a mad on at us for leaving him in the jungle, where he certainly deserves to be."

"And he is coming here?"

"Most definitely. As a matter of fact, I'm surprised that he isn't here already. You see, he was Natalya's, uh, boss, and we sort of dumped him. He is very likely to turn up angry, maybe even with reinforcements. We'd sure as hell better be ready for him, because he is one mean cat."

Hoon turned to Natalya. "Do you still work for him?"

"Of course not," she said. "I work for only one man." She smiled at him and he returned it.

"Then when Boris turns up we will shoot him," Hoon said. "No problem."

"Well, uh, Hoon," MacTavish said. "We want to avoid that if we can."

"Besides," Stratton said. "He wouldn't like it."

"He is a Soviet spy," said Fer-de-lance, narrowing his eyes and looking mean. "It is the breaks of the game. We ask no mercy. We give none."

"We'll see," said Hoon. "Keep an eye on the shoreline, both sides, and we'll try to see him first. Meanwhile, let's start the search."

In an hour Hoon had it organized. Runners ashore began loping down along the riverbanks, looking for an ordinary child's toy, hand-made and crude. Under the overhanging branches, two small, flat-bottomed boats poked into shallow places and behind rocks. It was the most dangerous part of the search because of the snakes which occasionally got into the trees and dropped—by accident or on purpose, into passing boats.

In the center of the narrow river, Hoon maneuvered the junk to keep it steady and motioned the various fishing boats to come alongside. When one appeared reluctant, he waved his rifle and smiled, then trained the gun on the boat. No one turned away.

By midday they had moved hardly more than a mile down the twisting river because of the many places to search. Hoon now slapped his forehead and cursed himself for being stupid. Soon he had a makeshift toy of the same size as the child's boat, and he put it in the water to see how the original toy boat might have drifted. But the second one got hung up on every small outcropping of the river bank, so he sent the runners back upriver in a small boat with orders to do it all over again. Finally, swearing, he took the whole operation back to its starting point and began again. Once or twice he searched the same fishing boats he had searched earlier, over the indignant protests of the owners.

By nightfall they had found nothing resembling what they were searching for. Hoon swung the bow around and at darkness they were within a hundred yards of where they had started from that morning. "We'll try again tomorrow," Hoon said.

"And will we try again tonight?" Natalya asked, smiling.

"Try? Try?"

"I am teasing."

"We will have to get to know you better."

"Yes," she said, moving against him. And dusk came again to the river, and the junk moved gently in the flowing water.

BANGKOK

The KGB *rezident* was not, as Boris believed, an idiot. Quite the contrary. The *rezident* was very clever.

Bangkok Station was a small office above a cabaret on Pat Pong Road. The road was famous in Asia, the cabaret indistinguishable from a thousand others. The *rezident* was female, aged, wrinkled, talented, and wry. She was small and wizened, but she wore expensive jade and sapphires as she sat at a very spartan writing desk. She smoked a foul-smelling Turkish cigar, having temporarily run out of the Havana panatelas she so enjoyed. She wore thick glasses and very expensive underwear. Her air was both Nina Ricci and one of competence.

The half of the room that she sat in was almost a copy of the typical Moscow office. It was spare and devoid of frills and sentiment, the nearest thing being a photo of Comrade Brezhnev in a hinged glass case. The walls, floor, ceiling, filing cabinet, and desk were all of the same moribund gray-green and they clashed with the splended Kelly-green Thai silk dress she wore.

She wrote at the spare desk with the nub of a pencil, marking laboriously on the thin Russian paper. She could have had supplies from the local market, much to be preferred, but she liked to keep herself in a Russian frame of mind when she dealt with her Russian bosses. She found it necessary to do that, to keep her identity safe and logical.

She wrote slowly, striving for precision because she wrote in English, her native language, and she wanted no errors when it was translated into Russian. She had long ago stopped making Shakespearean allusions, because once she almost sent the Red Army into battle over a phrase from *King Lear*.

SENDER: Bangkok Station. For: Chief, Four Section, KGB. D/T Grp 5141400. For Chief's eyes only. Relaying from Petrov.

Comrade! We salute you.

There is good news and bad news. First the good news: the Manchurian acrobatic team arrived and eventually made contact with Comrade Petrov. Now the bad news: there are four of them where once there were five. To explain.

You probably have seen their Flying Manchurian trick, where three of them build a quick launching platform and propel the fourth, who dives through a hoop held by the fifth and comes up after a forward roll and flip to land on his feet facing the audience. It was to prove unfortunate.

The team arrived in town and began to perform at various places. One of the places was a club, Le Château, on the 17th floor of a local hotel, where the champagne is not real, nor is the French accent of the maitre d' hôtel, who is a former Soho panhandler. But no matter.

The act was under way when several things happened at once, and by great coincidence. The pyramid was built and the Flying Manchurian went into his approach. He hit the pyramid/launching platform and was propelled with extreme velocity through the smoke-filled air of the club. At the same time, the fourth member of the team became slightly disoriented because of the reflecting lights in the club, and he held the hoop in a slightly different angle from the rehearsal. And also at the same time a waiter, responding to a request from a club patron (we have checked and the patron has no connection with American Intelligence; he is a Laplander who made a fortune peddling reindeer horn as an aphrodisiac)—the waiter opened a nearby window to let some of the smoke out.

So, the Flying Manchurian, with spectacular muscle control, was able to vector slightly from his flight path to pass through the hoop at the proper angle. He also passed through the open window.

Comrade, you would have been proud. Not a sound escaped his lips as he fell through the air.

Now, it so happened that on the street below was one of the many Indians who inhabit this city—you must remember our proximity to India—and this Indian was an Untouchable whose job it was to gather night soil (manure) and deliver it daily to a fertilizer factory on the edge of town. The Indian was driving his *ghari,* his cart, below the window when the Flying Manchurian made his most memorable flight. We were able to look down in time to see a small dark cloud arise above the open *ghari* and we knew the Flying Manchurian had finally completed his act. We cannot know the reaction of the Indian but he was, after all, an Untouchable, and it is quite likely he sized up the situation and simply kept going. He could not touch that which had plummeted into his cart, you see. At any rate, when we got to the street, the Indian, the *ghari,* and the acrobat were gone.

We can only surmise, at this point, that the acrobat has been spread over several acres of rice fields adjoining the city.

But on a cheerier note, the four remaining acrobats, who terminated their performance rather quickly following the swift and permanent exit of their fifth member, have at last been contacted by Comrade Petrov, who begs leave to report as follows—

He has taken the four acrobats and also recruited a handful of former soldiers from around town. At some personal expense, for which he hopes to be reimbursed, he has armed this force, amounting to about fifteen men, and taken them north.

For transport, Comrade Petrov has hired two helicopters by bribing the Air Force general in charge of such matters to take them north. Again, he hopes for reimbursement, as do I, for some of the funds he has used are budgeted for Bangkok Station, and as you probably know, Comrade, we are not excessively budgeted. Was it not Comrade Pushkin who wrote: *'Unhurt in northern blasts, the Russian rose will blow . . .'*

I mean, we will survive, Comrade.

It is Comrade Petrov's intention, in the north, to hire a boat (hoping, etc.) and come down the Mekong. His theory is that the stolen object will be somewhere near the river in the event the thieves tried to get across the border with it. The Laos border, as you may or may not know, is as secure as a sieve. Also, Comrade Petrov reasons that if the missing American mischief makers and the woman, Comrade Vorshova, who must be a prisoner, are to leave the country they will have to do so by boat.

The exact time Comrade Petrov will intercept the Americans and, possibly, the stolen object, is not known. It will depend on the river traffic, the type of boat he is able to rent (I am sure he will collect a receipt for future reimbursement), and other factors.

He had other message traffic for you, some of which I do not understand, but am merely relaying. He sends his respects to Comrade M_____; he says the lady whose photographs you have admired is no longer posing for art studies and is a disco lady in a Tokyo club, consequently, he will be sending you new photos at some point as you requested. He says he understands about Comrade Anya and will increase the square meters when he buys silk again.

Comrade Petrov certainly is hoping to wind this all up before he nears Cambodia, where, as you know, the fighting is more or less constant, and where he fears the Americans will somehow get caught up in it. So he is in great haste.

This is Bangkok Station, concluding. Remember Mother Russia.

Mother Russia, she sneered, putting down the pencil. *The last time I was in Mother Russia was forty years ago and I nearly froze my buns off in the damned snow.* At least it didn't snow in Thailand. *We face cobras, kraits, the monsoon, an occasional tiger, now and then a rogue elephant, periodic revolutions, and uncertain politics. But no snow.*

And Petrov, that numb-nut, the sooner he and his half-ass army were out of the country the sooner she could go back to her normal routine. She sighed. Time to earn a few *kip* from the other side.

Leaving the spartan side of the room, she took ten steps to the other side. The other side held a picture of the President's family, with the President in the center, in a non-glare glass case. There was a baby-blue file cabinet, a small coffee mess, and in the center of the half of the room, a chrome-and-laminated-wood monstrosity that was an American desk. It was enormous. To one side of it was a small typing stand and on the stand was an IBM Selectric II (correcting); against a far wall stood a small but dependable Xerox machine. She sat in an overstuffed swivel chair, executive model, and tried to get herself in an American frame of mind. The American half of the room helped. She leaned back for a few moments to collect her thoughts, then cranked into the typewriter a smooth sheet of bond paper which bore the seal of the U.S. embassy. It was time to divorce herself from the slate-gray Russian mentality and take on the false glamour of chrome. Time to be, as her passport stated, Kansas-born—and true-blue.

Kansas, she sneered again, ready to start writing. It was thirty years ago in Kansas that she had finally shed a husband, planted her last acre, put up her last Mason jar of tomatoes, and concluded there was damned little difference between the Russian and American peasantry and that she would not be either one. She had a good, quick, retentive mind and all things were possible. She smiled to herself; *most things had happened, too.* Then she turned her attention to typing the message.

CLASSIFICATION: Awfully secret.
ACTION PARTY: Addressee.
COPIES TO: Duty Officer, Originator
ORIGINATOR: Agent in Charge, Bangkok.
ADDRESSEE: Central Intelligence Agency.
MESSAGE:

At great personal risk have ascertained that the Russian agent, Boris Petrov, plus a handful of ex-soldiers and a five-man Manchurian acrobatic team (minus one) have confiscated two Thai helicopters in defiance of all international law and have gone north to recapture the stolen object. There are approximately fifteen men in his party.

I was able to detain them briefly through a ruse, but on your receipt of this message they probably will have arrived in the northeast.

It will be their intent to work down the Mekong in an attempt to intercept Fer-de-lance, who may or may not have the stolen object by now.

A noteworthy factor is the arrival in country of our people—The American Traveling Folk-Rock Five (ATFRF). I had anticipated their arrival, as discussed, with a certain amount of local publicity, and was able to get them booked into a club to add credence to their eventual trip north, in which they are to connect with Fer-de-lance. I must say that in all my years with the Agency here, I've never had a more difficult task than persuading the club management that these people are musicians. They seem incapable of playing the same song at the same time, and that 'O de doo dah day' stuff doesn't go over well here in Southeast Asia. Couldn't they have come out as a Mafia hit team?

But I must report on events which have ensued.

The team arrived and I had them give an impromptu performance at Don Muang Airport. Several things occurred simultaneously. Dogs began to howl. Two cows on the end of the runway galloped away, to the delight of the airport authorities, who had been trying to get rid of them. A tour group from Akron, Ohio stopped and applauded, but with some chauvinism, I suspect, because it was American, not because it was good. We had several complaints from the bar patrons and a rather precipitous clearing-out of the lounge area by other passengers. A saffron-robed priest jammed his begging bowl over his ears.

I don't know if you had a chance to hear them before they left. The one they call Black Snake has no sense of rhythm at all, and should never have been a bass player. Cobra's attempts at violin produced the kinds of sounds you normally associate with a two-car collision. Whoever told Cottonmouth he was a horn man has never met, seen or heard a horn man.

I won't go on. My purpose in stating all this is to acquaint you with the difficulties I had in arranging at least one booking for them here before we could logically send them on a country-wide tour.

I got them into a club called Le Château, on the 17th floor of a local hotel. The view is magnificent and the food, by American standards, is good. The club is a bit smokey, but what the hell.

The team's sole performance was to follow a rather energetic demonstration by the Manchurian acrobatic team, but they were a difficult act to follow. The show-stopper came when one Manchurian sailed out an open window on a final, silent swan-dive. When our people got up after that and began playing, waiters opened *all* the windows in hopes lightning would strike twice. When it became apparent nothing would happen, that the cacophony would continue, patrons were hurt in the rush to leave the club. The manager of Le Château, who has been useful to me from time to time, is very upset.

To conclude. The team did their one performance here and naturally we tried to get helicopters as well to get them upcountry. No luck. I sent them off in an old Land Rover which had been liberated by students from the British embassy. I trust they will make it, but not comfortably. They are a bit bewildered, I must add. Cobra, it turns out, is frightened to death of snakes. The best I could do was aim them in the right direction. I *did* admire their equipment; a banjo that can fire six hundred rounds a minute is technology at its finest.

I will continue to report, in triplicate as usual. Regards to my old friends in America.

All the friends I have anywhere are old, she thought. And then she smiled. *But some of them are still good. And I begin to appreciate them more and more.*

She finished and left with the messages. She would hand them to a go-go dancer who would pass them to a cab driver. The driver personally would encode the message to America and send it within the hour. The message to Russia would be entrusted to the driver's cousin, a silk-seller whose shop was near the Erawan. He, too would encode his message and dispatch it about the same time. She was very fair to both sides, and when she felt she had favored one over the other, she tried to make up for it the next time. She held several decorations from both Russian and American governments, which were grateful for her efforts.

She locked up and went down to the cabaret, where a succession of very pretty girls with very little bits of gauze were doing very naughty dances. To one of them, a saucy brunette, she handed the messages and left.

She rode in a cab through the streets of Bangkok to a quiet sector on the outskirts of Bangkok's Chinatown, passing *sam lor* drivers and a number of cinemas, passing tailor shops and small banks and Chinese restaurants. It was familiar territory.

Soon the cab stopped at a high-walled villa with a moon gate, and iron bars locked in front of the gate. She paid the driver and unlocked the bars and locked them again, passing through the moon gate and arriving at the entrance of her home.

It was, perhaps, the most expensive home in Bangkok. It had beams of teak, it had waterfalls and fountains, lily ponds and bamboo latticework. It had myriad rooms, and from one of them emerged an elderly Chinese gentleman in a loose, flowing robe of great quality and beauty. She greeted him with a hug; they had been living together for more than twenty-five years, and their love was uninhibited and total.

He led her gently into a small room which they regarded as the heart of their home. It was dimly lit, but cheerful, and it housed treasures of great value—Russian ikons and Ming vases and a fabulously old Chinese scroll which had been authenticated as a Wen Cheng-ming original.

The Chinese gentleman, whose name was Shen, clapped his hands once, softly, and a servant appeared with Chinese green tea. They sat at a small table and she began to relax, thanking the gods once again for having led her here, to Bangkok, and to Shen. They sipped their tea quietly and looked at each other with the calm affection that had taken them beyond being merely lovers when they were younger, to this plateau where they were the best of friends.

"And so," he said, "did you get your messages relayed?"

"One each. To both sides."

Shen stretched his back a little. "Let us hope they do not do too much damage to each other. Regretfully, we cannot stop them at this point."

"It probably would have been foolish to try. There would have been too many questions."

Shen nodded. "As usual, you are perceptive."

"And you, as usual, flatter me. I love it." They drank their tea in a short silence.

"Perhaps," Shen said, "they will not find each other?"

"They are such fools they will not be able to avoid it."

"Still," Shen said softly, "I do not as yet see any reason to tell my own people about it."

She considered it. "Maybe not."

Shen stretched again and poured more tea for the two of them and they sat for a while and contemplated their scroll, a beautiful mountain lake with snow on the mountains and a solitary fisherman on the lake.

"It is *very* Chinese," she said at last.

"Yes."

"How do you think," she asked, suddenly shifting back to the night's work, "those idiots would feel if they knew this was all for nothing?"

Shen smiled. It make him look younger. "It would be amusing to tell them," he said. "To simply assemble them in a room and say to them, 'Gentlemen, the People's Republic of China long ago found those stupid bombs and dismantled them'!"

She laughed aloud.

"But we must let them go through with it," Shen said. "Otherwise, they will know too much, or suspect too much. Too many people would be endangered later. We could be threatened by it."

"So we let them play their game," she nodded.

"Yes. We cannot let the world know of the relationship the three superpowers have had in Asia for the past three decades—a relationship contained in this one room." Shen smiled at her. "And does it still excite you?"

She nodded again. "Just as you still excite me, my dear."

Much later, when the tea had cooled, they turned out the light in the small room and walked through their sanctuary to the bedroom where, as they had for so many years, they fell asleep in the large teak bed, and in each other's arms.

THE RIVER

Hoon's crew found him to be much more mellow now that the Russian girl was aboard, but it was a mistake to push his good humor too far. One or two of them had found the search for the golden junk tiresome and had been found taking an unauthorized midday nap, only to feel the thud of his boot and the lash of his tongue.

They were into the third day and had worked only two miles down the river. "At this rate," observed Hoon, "we only have eight months to go before we're back in the South China Sea. Care to spend the next eight months doing this?"

Natalya was sympathetic. Stratton's patience was wearing extremely thin. Fer-de-lance suddenly had blossomed into the compleat professional and *he* was willing to spend as much time as necessary on the river. His soft pink skin was acquiring a beige tinge and he seemed to be holding himself straighter. He noticed that some of his pot was disappearing, too, and the old, rakehell feeling was growing stronger than ever.

It was MacTavish, though, who came up with the idea of recruiting the villages' children to help with the search. It came to him one day when he was watching two small boys fishing from the bank, and surrounded by other kids. "Listen," he told Hoon. "If there's one thing Southeast Asia has, it's kids. Let's put them to use."

So they had sent runners into all the villages, gathering the children around and making a game of it, and offering a fat reward. The children jumped at the adventure, and all down the river they were searching the areas close to the villages. It was the sectors between villages that now occupied Hoon and the others, and it was just as tedious as the first day had been. Twice they had disturbed lovers in boats under the overhanging trees. Once a snake had plopped into the water alongside the boat, sending two Portuguese sailors into near-hysteria.

It was Hoon, with his hawk's eyes, who finally spotted the golden junk.

It came early in the morning, soon after sunup, when they were all on deck and contemplating yet another day on the cramped boat. Hoon reacted to a quick glint from the shoreline to his left, a glint he thought might come from metal, such as a rifle barrel. He watched it without seeming to watch it, but he never saw it again. Then he realized the spot where he saw it was so low in the water that it couldn't be a weapon, unless it was a submarine a long way from home. But it was definitely made of metal.

Casually he called over two of his crewmen, pointed to the spot and said calmly, yet loud enough for all to hear: "Paddle over there and pick up the thing, will you? It will be in the wooden boat, probably with the overhead missing, just under the overhang of that tree with the dead moss in it." The crewmen gaped at him.

"Move it," he said, and turned to find the others staring in disbelief. "What the hell," he said. "It had to turn up somewhere."

"At last," breathed Natalya. MacTavish, Farley, and Stratton gripped the gunwales and watched in silence as the two sailors hurried to the spot. They swung the small boat around the overhang of the tree, and with a shout, went directly for the shoreline.

They emerged almost immediately, their excited laughter ringing clearly over the water. One of them held aloft the model of an Asian junk, not more than ten inches long and with a spreading golden lateen sail, and it gleamed brightly in the sunlight.

"You baboon's ass," Hoon yelled. "If you drop it you will never make love again."

The sailor quickly sat back and cradled the junk in his arms, and Hoon laughed, throwing back his head and letting go with great roaring sounds that were part amusement, part relief. In a moment the others were laughing, too.

The two sailors came alongside and Hoon reached down very carefully and lifted up the junk. It was not as heavy as he had thought it might be, and he saw that the gold was not massive but thin and well shaped to the exact likeness of a trading junk. Except for a small bit of dirt, it was in wonderful shape, and he marveled at the delicacy of the work.

He could feel the others crowding around him, and he held it aloft, watching it catch the sun. Nothing on the outside of it indicated any sort of map or directions. That would be on the inside, probably molded into the hulls.

"Well," he grinned, "and what am I bid?" and he turned to look at Farley. Farley started to answer and stopped, staring at MacTavish, who was transfixed, looking upriver.

"Oh, shit," MacTavish whispered. They spun around to look.

Two junks were descending on them, one on each side. The left one was bristling with a motley-looking crew; the right junk held some crewmen and a group of splendid-looking athletes. And amidships, Boris stood glaring at them, his face both angry and triumphant.

Before anyone else could react, Hoon had his knife out and was slashing at the mooring lines. Stratton and MacTavish, moving simultaneously, ran into each other and bounced back, instantly angry. Natalya wheeled and headed for the cabin where Hoon's rifle lay on an unused bunk.

Farley's reaction was to stare. Here, at last, was the enemy. The real, tangible, and very impressive enemy, bearing down on them and brandishing weapons. The big Caucasian waving a large pistol in their general direction must be Boris. For a split second Farley analyzed his feelings. He knew a deep-down fear but could handle it. He also felt a sudden surge of excitement as the junks loomed closer. He began to grin. He had never felt more alive in his life.

"You bastards," he yelled in his high-pitched voice, "come and get it!" And with that he tugged at the button on his left shirt-flap. When he had gotten it free he ran toward the bow of the junk, but at that moment Hoon had hauled the tiller over and the junk was free in the river current. It began to swing, so Farley stopped, turned, and lunged back toward the stern, where he ran headlong into Natalya and knocked her flat on the deck, the rifle clattering noisily back down the ladder of the cabin she had just left. Without wasting a word she clambered up and started for the rifle again, then stopped to stare at the little American as he positioned himself in the stern, drew back his right arm, and let fly with the shirt button.

The button arched through the still morning air and the moment seemed to hang there forever. In the stillness they could hear Farley quietly counting, "one—two—three—four—"

MacTavish saw Boris raise his pistol. There was a flash and a roar and a geyser of debris erupted over Boris's junk; the shock wave caught the stern of their own junk and picked it out of the water and dropped it flatly back into the river. Hoon's delighted laughter rang through the sound of falling water and the echoes of the explosion.

When they could see again, Boris and most of the junk's crew were in the water. Hoon was nearly hysterical with laughter, and it infected Natalya, who leaned against the deckhouse and began to shake.

"Good show, Bonde," Stratton said clearly.

"I told you," Farley said. "It's Farley. Henderson Farley. Remember the name."

"Christ," MacTavish said wonderingly, "he's become a tiger."

Suddenly they felt the engine kick to life and the surge as the junk started downriver under power. Behind them, the undamaged junk had stopped and was fishing Boris and the others out of the river. Hoon looked around his own junk, appraising the situation with a deliberate eye. They were badly outnumbered; it was time to cut and run downriver and perhaps lay in ambush around some bend. It was better than trying to outshoot them now, even with some of them in the water.

He yelled and his men leaped to the sails. Even a little wind might help the straining engine, which to Hoon sounded as if it were on its last legs. He longed for the river mouth and his magnificent *lorcha,* which would outsail anything; he would love to give them a fight from the decks of his own ship. Natalya watched him, marveling at his strength and sureness, at the cruelty in his dark face, when he could be so gentle—

"Natalya!" He was gesturing for her and she moved to stand beside him. He put his arm around her and smiled down at her, and she stood looking at him as the junk moved downriver.

MacTavish watched them now with no jealousy at all. If ever a pair were matched, there they were. *The human condition,* he thought. *We turn a corner and there she is, or we turn a corner and she will be a half-hour late, and we've gone. Ah, Wan Chai, Fu Manchu Two, Chow Fun, when this is over I'm coming home for good. Well, maybe for a long while. Who knows?*

"This isn't over yet," Farley said suddenly, as if reading his thoughts. "What's the plan, Hoon? Let's *us* attack *them.*"

"Ambush," Hoon said quietly.

"I like that," Farley nodded.

Stratton, meanwhile, was standing in the stern of the junk, looking back upriver. He was exultant. *I have been in combat and lived to tell about it. And boy, will I tell about it. None of those desk jockeys can match this experience.* He could see the promo for the series now: *"Combat-tested Sidney Stratton, the distinguished correspondent and Asian expert, gives the inside story . . ."* Unless that drunken sod, MacTavish, got it into print first. Well, no matter. He could pull it off.

Hoon gave a final glance back. They had outdistanced the remaining junk, which was still pulling people out of the river. Given a little luck they could round a bend, get ashore, and rake the onrushing junk from the river bank. He looked quickly downriver. Yes, it might be possible. He turned to look again at Natalya, whose face was alive with excitement. One in a million. He smiled at her, the smile on the face of a wolf.

"I think I love you," he said.

She threw her arms around him, holding him very close and very tight as the junk made the swift turn around the bend. She was still holding him when the collision came.

Cobra had been carsick on the way to the airport in a hell-for-leather Washington cab; he had been ill on the airplane. The blanket of humidity thrown over him when he stepped from the plane at Don Muang had depressed him even more than the en route briefing. The jolting Land Rover that had taken them as far as Khon Kaen, before being stolen from them, had done irreparable harm to his kidneys. But the cultural shock of Asia had wounded him, perhaps mortally. The sights and smells had been overpowering. The language difficulties had added to the problems.

His companions were scarcely better off. Cottonmouth had developed a severe allergy to almost everything Asian, and the rest of the team believed it was all psychological, and while Black Snake could handle the heat and humidity, he hated the food. The fourth member, a perspiring little man who was substituting for Water Moccasin (who had slipped in his bath and broken a leg, some said deliberately)—the fourth member was Rattlesnake, who had thrown up with fine regularity since eating Thai ice cream in a little market town outside Bangkok. When not throwing up, he was squatting in the jungle, starting at every noise and straining to be as quick as possible to get out of the bush.

When the Land Rover was stolen at Khon Kaen they had veered to the right and ridden a bus to the Mekong. It was a never-to-be-forgotten experience, for the upper chrome of the old Mercedes bus contained a quantity of heroin that would make the driver rich if it were delivered safely and on time. Consequently, the bus had careened off embankments, struck a *sam lor* without stopping, terrified all inside, and finally arrived, wheezing, at the border town. Cobra and his crew spilled out of the bus on shaky legs and threw themselves gratefully on Mother Earth. It was a long time before they worked up the nerve to stage a performance as a way of maintaining their cover and attracting enough attention to rent a boat and start upriver.

The boat owner had fallen asleep in the stern, and Rattlesnake had taken the tiller. The other three took turns pumping with the antiquated bailing system, for it became alarmingly clear that the boat would not go a mile without constant pumping. They had taken turns on the pump, followed by their turns at hanging over the stern because of their collective diarrhea, and in a short time had gotten the system down to an enervating routine. Generally, it was a silent routine. Their aggrieved nervous systems, the strangeness of the experiences, their perceived dangers, all worked to keep them downcast and brooding.

Only once in the past few minutes had Cobra spoken. "We're running out of toilet paper," he said gloomily.

"But we can't turn back," he added, when no one else spoke. "Hurry on to the next village. Can't this dreadful thing go any *faster?*"

He turned his back on the river, where he had been acting

as lookout for the river debris, and walked over to stand above the snoring boat owner. *"Do get up,"* he urged. "We could be in trouble."

The boat owner shifted and sat up. "Who's watching the river?" he asked, but no one understood him. He was just getting to his feet when the collision came.

There was a tremendous banging noise followed by the unmistakable sound of splintering wood. The two junks rose out of the water slightly and settled back, locked together by their shattered bows. Everything loose on both vessels pitched forward except for Cottonmouth, who had been squatting, pants down, over the stern of the boat. Cottonmouth made a neat if unplanned arc and plummeted into the river.

Cobra was thrown forward and bounced off the deck housing. He landed heavily, face down, near the splintered bow. He raised his head and stared; two feet away from him was Fer-de-lance, also flat on the deck, and gaping at him.

"Farley!" screamed Cobra.

"You incompetent bastard," Fer-de-lance said coldly. "You'll work the night shift forever."

Black Snake, too, had been pitched forward, and in midair collided with an evil-looking pirate, both falling into the mangled bows of both junks, bows which resembled a small sawmill more than two boats. Natalya and Hoon, still locked, had slammed into the junk's mast and fallen heavily to the deck, but as Hoon painfully got up he could see Natalya was also rising, apparently bruised but not seriously hurt. He looked quickly toward the stern; MacTavish and Stratton, who had been standing there, were now forward, and slowly getting to their feet. One of his crewmen was in the water.

"Stop the engine," Hoon yelled. "Cut the sail free." He saw crewmen leap to his command and he turned his attention back to the mess in front of him. It was a confusion of people, splintered wood, lines, a dropped sail, and people yelling in half a dozen languages.

"Quiet," he yelled again, knowing he had to take quick

command to get the boats apart or get off before they sank. In the sudden silence that followed he was aware of another noise: a small, thumping gasoline engine.

Even as he realized what it was, he was spinning around. And even as he turned it was too late. The junk bearing Boris and his henchmen rammed at full speed into the stern of Hoon's junk.

Again there was the jolt of impact, and more crewmen splashed into the water. Boris's gun flew out of his hand and over the side as his junk shuddered to a halt, and Boris himself hit the deck and skidded forward to bang into the small deckhouse.

The Flying Manchurians reacted superbly. Thrown forward by the impact, they hit and rolled, and came up as if on springs, appraising the situation even as they came upright. What they saw was three boats joined as if a giant child had reached down and crammed them all together; the second impact had locked them in a welter of twisted wood. Engines had stalled, and now all three battered boats were drifting downriver in the running current.

In the few heartbeats that followed, everyone reacted. The great Mekong River battle was joined.

Boris rolled forward, a bear of a man, sweeping men aside like straw dummies, looking for the golden junk. The roustabout soldiers he had recruited locked in hand-to-hand fighting with Hoon's crewmen, all knowing it was too close quarters to use a weapon at risk of hitting your friends and missing your enemies.

Natalya stood on deck with a splintered spar from the sail, swinging it with more enthusiasm than skill, but totally unafraid.

Hoon, using all the kung fu he had picked up in Hong Kong, was cutting a swath through the charging ruffians from Boris's junk.

Stratton stood very calmly and walked through the middle of the melee, observing. He was trying to see it as his cameraman might see it, so he could "reconstruct" it for the benefit of his audience. Like a man with a charmed life, he moved with some dignity through the fighting and remained untouched

MacTavish was engaged in an old-style bar brawl with two of Boris's crewmen near the stern of Hoon's junk. That personal war was conducted with great swinging of arms and much panting, but little damage was inflicted by anyone.

Fer-de-lance moved with cold precision through the yelling, fighting crowd, pausing occasionally to jab or kick as he found an opportunity. Like Stratton, he was strangely untouched by the violence around him.

Black Snake was swinging his bass with a kind of studied nonchalance, but causing damage when he connected; Cottonmouth, who had lost his pants in the tumble from the stern, was back on deck and trying to wrap a portion of the torn sail around him and fight off one of Boris's recruits at the same time; it was not the best position to be in during a fight.

The Flying Manchurians were magnificent. Hitting and bounding, they were taking their toll of Hoon's crewmen, then executing beautiful gymnastic rolls and leaps to get clear to strike at another point. It became clear that through their efforts, Boris and his henchmen slowly were winning the battle.

Hoon decided to take them out. He worked his way aft and picked up a shattered board, kicking a man who tried to stop him. He stalked the Manchurian who had just chopped down one of his crewmen, and as the Flying Manchurian went into a forward roll to get clear, Hoon started a mighty swing. The result was devastating. The board caught the Flying Manchurian in midair and sent him, like a booming triple, over the gunwales and into the water. Hoon grinned and looked for the next one.

The second Manchurian was in a dead run, preparing for a forward roll also, to bring himself up behind one of Hoon's men who was grappling with Boris. As the Manchurian began his run, Hoon shoved the board between his legs. The

Manchurian went down like a felled tree and skidded forward. He went through the sprung door of the deckhouse and hit every step that led downward into Hoon's cabin. Hoon glanced in and saw the Flying Manchurian crashed at the foot of the ladder.

The third Manchurian had singled out Stratton and was charging the newsman's back when Stratton turned and stepped aside, apparently lost in thought. The Manchurian went screaming over the side and into the water, and was last seen threshing around as the junks continued their inexorable drift downriver in the clutch of the current.

As the junks drifted they spun slowly around in the water. It was difficult to keep footing on the moving deck in the midst of the noise and confusion. MacTavish staggered once, having missed a roundhouse punch, and straightened up again to study the situation. As he glanced around he saw the bottle of scotch.

It apparently had been dropped by some crewman, but was intact. *It is an omen,* MacTavish thought. *The gods have spoken.* MacTavish stooped and reached for the scotch as the last remaining Flying Manchurian hurtled across the deck at him. The compact, wiry body caught the corner of MacTavish's eye and he instinctively brought the bottle down to protect it. There was a shattering crash and shards of bottle flew everywhere as the Flying Manchurian dropped as if he had smashed into a stone wall. MacTavish looked in astonishment at the neck of the bottle still in his hand, and then glared in a great anger at the still form of the Manchurian acrobat. He knew a cold fury. "You inhuman son of a bitch," he said to the unconscious form.

The tide had turned, both on the decks of the battered boats and in the sweep of the river. The Mekong had widened, then narrowed, and forced the wrecks into the eddy of some large rocks. On board, the hired hands that Boris had found in Bangkok suddenly began deserting the fray. Without the Manchurians, they were almost leaderless.

Almost, except for Boris.

With the confusion on deck beginning to sort itself out, Hoon and Boris instinctively looked for the opposition leadership. Their eyes met and locked across twenty feet of deck, and they moved slowly toward each other. Natalya stopped, half in fear and half in wonder, as the two men closed in on each other.

Boris feinted and Hoon kicked him expertly in the stomach. The big Russian grunted and stepped back, then closed again and managed to grab Hoon's arm and spin him around in an armlock. But Hoon dropped to the deck and Boris lost his hold, and as the Russian reached again, Hoon chopped his wrist and twisted away.

On their feet again the two men charged, Boris trying to seize Hoon in a fatal bear hug. Hoon went under and cracked Boris across the face with his elbow. The Russian staggered and Hoon hit him again. Boris flew back against a shattered mast and immediately rolled forward, knocking Hoon off his feet. Hoon sprang up just in time to see the big Russian bearing down on him at full speed.

The boats turned again. Boris had no way of knowing an overhanging tree branch would suddenly appear. As Hoon braced himself for the attack, Boris ran headlong into the branch. It sounded like the collision of two hurtling trains.

The impact knocked Boris backward and off the boat. He hit the dirty water of the Mekong and sank like a rock, but in a few minutes they saw him bob up again. He started to swim for the boats, but now the river had caught them again and the jammed-together hulks swirled out in the mainstream of the river and began to move rapidly away. As Boris dropped further and further back, Hoon's crewmen began throwing his hired gang over the side.

Hoon whirled. In his first glance he saw MacTavish and Stratton, and he heared Natalya saying something behind him. He found Farley kicking the last of Boris's henchmen over the gunwales. The strange new Americans seemed to be gathering near the stern, and they looked in fair shape. He began to grin, then stopped abruptly and raced down to the cabin. A Flying Manchurian was just waking up at the foot of the ladder. Hoon started manhandling him up the ladder; willing hands pulled him the rest of the way. Hoon heard them pitch him overboard.

He turned back to the cabin. The bed, where he and Natalya had learned much from each other, was intact. In the middle of it the golden junk lay undamaged, the light playing along the sail and exquisite curve of the hull. Topside again, he surveyed the damage. It was considerable. Natalya moved to stand beside him, and put her hand up on his shoulder. He looked down at her beautiful face, with the slight bruise on one cheek.

"So you want to be a pirate," he said, touching her hair softly. She hugged him tightly.

"Well then, we must get you out of here and on a proper pirate ship, my little *malasada.*" He looked up again. The hulls would sink before they could get downriver, even if Boris did not make another effort, which he might. The thing to do now was go inland, steal a jeep or two, and make it to the mouth of the Mekong and his waiting *lorcha.* He turned his face to the wind; he was greatly pleased with this adventure, with the golden junk and the golden girl. He began to laugh.

All aboard the wrecked junks heard Hoon's sudden laughter, and were caught up in it. Even MacTavish, still upset at the loss of the scotch, began to come around. After all, there would be other scotches. Stratton, as if reading his thoughts, suddenly began to talk of a rum and Coke in the Journalists' Club in Hong Kong. And Farley, his anger at Cobra forgotten in the thrill of victory, moved forward to talk with Hoon. They still had to settle the matter of the golden junk. He was sure they could; Uncle Sam was a big spender.

LANGLEY

The Deputy Director, Covert and Clandestine Activities, Central Intelligence Agency, hurried down the wide tiled hallway toward his office. His head throbbed with both the echo of last night's cocktail party conversation and the strong *kava* he had drunk at the Tongan Embassy. It had been a strain; the *kava* was powerful and stealthy, and the cover role he had had to play made great demands. He had turned up at the party as a Catholic priest, because the Agency's information was that the Tongans were religious people. He had worn the robes because he felt that as a man of the cloth he could pick up any official secrets. When he got to the party he learned quickly that almost all Tongans were Methodists. In the end he had found himself in amiable conversation with a bearded Russian who said he was a Russian Orthodox priest, but who didn't seem to know much about religion. The priest had kept asking him whether he knew if there was a deep-water harbor in Tonga, obviously in the mistaken belief that he had visited Tonga at one time or another. Why would a priest care about that sort of thing?

He reached his office and eased himself into the swivel chair and closed his eyes for a while. When he opened them again he discovered that an hour had passed, and someone had put a folder on his desk. Damn! Who had caught him sleeping? He reached for the folder and sat back to read.

CLASSIFICATION: Don't Even Whisper It.

ACTION PARTY: Addressee.

COPIES TO: Duty Officer, Librarian.

ORIGINATOR: Henderson (Fer-de-lance) Farley, Agent-in-Charge, Supplemental Unit, Infiltration & Tactics (SUIT).

ADDRESSEE: Deputy Director, Covert and Clandestine Activities, Central Intelligence Agency, Langley, Virginia.

MESSAGE:

Sighted Ship, Secured Same!

At long last we have recovered the golden junk. I am happy to report that it is secure in the safe of our Hong Kong office, and will be hand-carried by diplomatic courier home to America. God Bless America! If anything will make you appreciate your own country, it's spending a lot of time hunkering in an Asian jungle.

To summarize: Following my briefing in Honolulu I was passed through our people and on into Indochina. After securing the necessary equipment, I made a carefully planned incursion into what we thought was the proper village on the curve of the Mekong River near the Lao border. There we encountered certain difficulties, notably the language barrier. When I walked through the village streets I tried to get help from the local girls, but they only wanted to sell me trinkets. The native men were suspicious at first and I thought I might have to subdue one or two of them, but it turned out all right, and I learned we were too far upriver. By process of elimination I got the helicopter pilot to the right village but not, I'm afraid, until we had inadvertently blown the roofs off a lot of village huts up and down the river. I understand we may be getting a bill for the damages, but I assure you it was unavoidable—we had to fly low to see anything.

176

By what I must modestly say was rather shrewd deduction, we arrived at the right village and I hired a boat to take me down the Mekong. On the river I encountered what was obviously a party of pirates, and by pretending to go along with them, at last made my way to the Old One, the guru who had disposed of the golden junk. Following my brisk interrogation of the guru, I was able to establish the general area of the river which held the junk and, enlisting the aid of the pirates, I recovered it from its hiding place.

At that moment we were attacked by a tremendous party of Russian hirelings headed by a notorious KGB agent, Boris Ivanovich Petrov (see Four Section, 1st Directorate file if Miss Brumley can find it). It was obvious from Boris's actions and the large gun he was pointing that he intended to "inflict the highest measure of punishment," as the KGB so quaintly puts it. I was forced to rely on the buttonbombs that Roscoe had sewn onto my jacket, and later also forced to rely on my martial arts skill. With a little help from the pirates I was able to vanquish the attacking hordes, and at last sight, most were bobbing around in the muddy Mekong.

I did appreciate the help provided by the remainder of my unit (SUIT), although I have to say I probably could have handled it alone. The joint effort, however, did instill a sense of camaraderie, and I hope the Agency will see fit to keep us intact and operational.

I will be returning to America on earliest transportation and submitting a more detailed report.

Oh, yes—the bad news. Through the ineptness of the KBG agent, two newsmen were along for most of the events. You may or may not be seeing this same report, probably in exaggerated versions, on the tube and in print. Sorry about that. The other piece of bad news is that due to overwhelming odds, the golden junk remained in the hands of the damned pirates until I offered them money for it. I'm afraid I had to promise them a lot more money than had been authorized, but there was no way out other than termination with extreme prejudice, which could have been messy. So the pirate, Hoon, wants you to send a cashier's check to his bank in Macau or he'll tell the world what he saw inside the hull of the golden junk. I think we'd better play ball with him, for now.

Incidentally, before leaving Thailand I had the opportunity to meet and talk with our agent-in-charge in Bangkok. What a professional! She is doing a great job against tremendous odds and with an inadequate budget. Her knowledge of affairs in both Russia and The People's Republic of China is nothing short of phenomenal, and if we can see our way clear to give her more money or a decoration of some sort, or both, it would certainly be in our best interests.

EPILOGUE

Natalya, wearing only the bottom half of a string bikini, stretched and yawned on the terrace of Hoon's villa in Macau. *Their* villa. Since their meeting, since the battle on the junks and the trek to a nearby village, since the arrival aboard his *lorcha* and the journey to Macau, she knew they would be sharing a future.

They had no secrets now. She told him everything. Lying in his arms she had talked of her mother, a beauty contest winner in Irkutsk, and her father, a Moscow doctor. She had talked about being in the Young Pioneers and how her father had used *blat*, influence, to get her into the special High School Number Three where the children of *nomenklatura* bigwigs were educated. She talked about graduation from Moscow University and subsequent English language training and translating articles from *Pravda, Izvestia* and *Red Star*. It was hardly the usual impoverished childhood and adolescence, but the thoughts of greater adventure whetted her appetite and the assignments abroad that had followed made her life interesting, even thrilling. And now Hoon. He was the *compleat* adventurer and he didn't even snore. The perfect man, the perfect life—especially now that they were incredibly rich. She turned on her stomach and felt the welcome sun on her back and the slight breeze coming off the ocean. Life couldn't be better. For a moment, but only for a moment, she wondered what had happened to Boris . . .

Boris was shaking in the winter cold. Even indoors, the Siberian weather was enough to make strong men quake, and like the chief of Four Section, he wore his greatcoat while sitting at his desk. Occasionally, but not often, he thought of Paris, of white thighs and sparkling champagne. *But that way madness lies.*

He looked around the stark room he shared with his chief. It was made gloomier by the fact that the chief and his stupid cow of a wife, Anya, refused to talk to him. They thought it was his fault they were here. How could he tell them the tremendous odds he had been up against, or the fact that the Flying Manchurians were little help? The only bright spot in the entire operation was that after the failure of the mission, the KGB *rezident* in Bangkok turned out to be so competent. She had been a tremendous help with the Thai police, and had gotten things under control and Boris out of the country. But for her he might be spending years in some filthy cell. He had recommended her for more money and a decoration.

He felt the wind hammering against the walls and heard the house creak. The snow was piled high against the outside and a few nights earlier he had heard wolves howling in the line of trees near their lonely building. He dreaded the walk to the outdoor privy but he had to go. He turned up his collar and stepped out into the stinging wind and blowing snow. Damned pirate. If he ever again got his hands on Hoon . . .

Hoon stood on the deck of his *lorcha* with the Paracel Islands falling away to the stern and his course slightly east of Macau to take advantage of the winds. He had all sails set and his quick, rakish craft was hull down for Macau and Natalya. He ached for the beauteous Russian girl with all his mind and body. In the months she had been with him she had become a total part of his life, and he lighted joss sticks in gratitude to whatever gods had led her to him. She had made him a complete man.

He had no secrets from her. He told her about Macau in the early days when he learned how to cheat in the Mah Jongg parlors. Later, when he had learned that Chinese residents were forbidden to enter the gambling casinos, he had forged them tourist identification cards made more authentic with his stolen plastic laminating machine. Eventually Hoon was able to hire a forger who could supply fake death certificates to Chinese families in the Chinese wards so they could collect insurance proceeds from Portuguese insurance companies in the International ward. Hoon was not prejudiced, and he took only ten percent from clients in each of the wards. He became an apprentice smuggler and made his way down to the Kra peninsula and hooked up with Thai pirates. He smuggled cigarettes into Mindanao and transistor radios to Nationalist Chinese troops on Quemoy. But eventually he got his *lorcha* and fell in love with the wild and quixotic sea, and now he ranged over the ocean in pure enjoyment. He knew his base was secure, because the selling of the golden junk to the strange little American had made him one of the richest men in Asia. Occasionally he wondered what had happened to the American . . .

Fer-de-lance sat behind his desk in a new and well-appointed office on the fourth floor of the building in Langley, Virginia. He, too, had a wide-angle view of the Potomac valley, a view he enjoyed from behind the massive desk. The sign on his door still identified him as Chief of Supplemental Unit, Infiltration and Tactics, except when visitors came and the sign had to be covered by the bamboo drapes he had brought back from his Hong Kong stopover. The unit was very hush-hush now, so much so that few in the building knew what Farley's duties and responsibilities were. Farley himself had only a vague idea, and much of his time was spent advising Miss Brumley where to put files and in trying to get a parking space closer to the building.

The unit had prospered because the mission had succeeded. The deadly Fer-de-lance had pulled off a coup when all about him had expected failure. They had sent him to Asia because he and his unit were expendable, nothing more than a holding action until the heavyweights could get ready. But he had come back with his troops intact and the golden junk safe in hand.

Subsequently, his government had notified the People's Republic of China of the dreadful mistake that had been made, and the Chinese government responded with great wisdom and courtesy, though not without a few demands. Most of the demands had been met but there were a few exceptions; America would not surrender the formula for Coca-Cola concentrate, for example, but negotiations had proceeded in other directions and relations were fairly smooth.

The bottom line was Fer-de-lance in a new and spacious office and his old organization, except for that damned Adder, elevated to positions of pay and power they had not dreamed of earlier. Their eighteen years of training were viewed by the rest of the Agency as remarkably patient and persevering, readying them for their extraordinary mission. All was forgiven and Cobra had even gotten a day shift. Farley was content, probably even more content than that television fellow, Stratton, whom Farley had met by accident at a Georgetown cocktail party. . .

Stratton wore his new experiences well, after the first initial shock in Bangkok following the completion of their ordeal, as he liked to think of it. The shock was that somehow the word had leaked out and there *they* were like a pack of wolves—the damned Press. Hoon, Natalya, even the little American spy had managed to slip away, but the reporters and photographers had surrounded Stratton and MacTavish and started firing cameras and questions. Well, it was to be expected; after all he, Stratton, was an internationally-known reporter and commentator, as much a news-maker as a news reporter. He had thrust out his famous chin and talked about the savage trek through the jungle, the menacing KGB *apparat* and its evil henchmen dogging their footsteps. He talked about the golden junk and how he had led the search for it, and about his leadership in the great river battle which followed.

Viewers around the world saw the telecast. A disheveled but still distinguished Sidney Stratton, firm and forceful, looked straight into the camera, establishing good eye contact, and talked with authority about the wild adventure in Asia. In the background a rumpled man in a filthy bush jacket kept jumping up and waving his arms and shouting, "no . . . no . . . all bullshit . . . not like that at all . . ." until someone subdued him and got him out of camera range. Much later, when MacTavish's stories ran in newspapers around the world, Stratton was asked why he had not mentioned the bombs in the Great Wall of China. He had lowered his head and talked regretfully about the tendency of the Press to ignore national interests and national security for the sake of a sensationalized story.

From time to time Stratton reminded his audiences that he had personally taken part in a great mission in an Asian jungle, implying that a good reporter sometimes had to go *inside* to bring back the story, to get involved in the dirt and danger. As he was saying the other day to a certain Prime Minister, "P.M., you've got to mingle a little with the herd if you want to know where the manure is coming from." The P.M. was properly impressed and properly grateful. The only fly in Stratton's honey was MacTavish, whose own account of the story differed wildly from Stratton's. But Stratton was sure that his version would be the one finally accepted by the masses. After all, the ratings had shown that his credibility factor was the highest on network news. And with his promotion and new honors, including tea in the Oval Office, he could afford to ignore a pipsqueak like MacTavish . . .

Lying on his back on a Wan Chai dock, MacTavish was trying to navigate by the stars. A *taxi-wallah* had gotten him to the edge of the ocean and now it was up to him to prove his theory, which was: if you went due east of Hong Kong, and if you went far enough, you would end up back in Wan Chai. It was what he kept trying to tell that twitchy little girl from Reuters as they were getting into bed, but she didn't seem to care. Well, he cared. He cared about everything that started or stopped in Hong Kong.

So now it was up to him. Which way was east? He would wait until sunup because a popular song in Asia was "The East is Red," and he would head toward the first pink tendrils in the sky. He was very pleased with himself. You had to be clever to survive in Wan Chai.

Chow Fun suddenly loomed over him. "By Jesus Christ, by Joe Namath, by Ernest Hemingway. . ."

"Shut up, Chow Fun. I'm dead-reckoning my way across the wine-dark sea."

"Listen, MacTavish. Fu Manchu Two want you."

"Umf."

"He say come now. Buy you plenty whiskey. He very happy. You write about his place, good business."

"Yeah, okay. But then I'm goin' around the world and end up in Wan Chai."

"You awready in Wan Chai."

"Don't you understand? *Because it's there!*"

"Come on, MacTavish. I help you up."

"What happened to the girl from Reuters? The brunette with the mole on her. . ."

"She wait for you. She and Fu Manchu Two. Come."

MacTavish lurched to his feet and leaned on his little Chinese friend. He felt a great affection for Chow Fun, and it was followed by a moment of blinding clarity. "I am," he explained, "one of the last free men, Chow Fun. I drink a little, I screw around a little. But I write better than old Stratton talks. I don't lie, and I don't take any shit from anyone."

"Okay, MacTavish," Chow Fun agreed.

"You're damned right it's okay," MacTavish said standing as straight as possible under the circumstances. And the two old friends, laughing, padded through the Hong Kong night . . .

In an upcountry Thai village near the Mekong, it was night as well. The Old One had spent a pleasant day giving advice to some of the villagers who wanted to go over into Laos to court the Laotian girls. It was a situation with a lot of ramifications, and he had enjoyed working out the solution. Now he sat in the darkness and listened to the noises. Some were menacing, some comforting, but all were familiar and that was what his peace of mind demanded.

Since Pim had run off with the American sailor he had tried to arrange his life so there were no more surprises. Even the intrusions of the pirates and the Americans, and later the Russian and his hired guns, had made him more philosophical, and he had found it a tactical advantage not to be surprised. If you never admitted to surprise, you would never be surprised. He hoped he could remember that for the next visit of neighboring village headman.

He wondered how the affair of the golden junk had turned out. Sooner or later someone would drop by and tell him. Until then, he had other things to do.

In the distance he heard the rain begin. It would sweep over Southeast Asia like something alive, hurled from the gray and ominous clouds. Then the clouds would disappear and the sun would come, warm and life-giving and consistent. It was as it should be.

The Old One lay down on the mat and closed his eyes.